Lock Down Publications and Ca$h
Presents

I0637439

PROBLEM SOLVED 3

Play Time is Over

Written By
Christopher "Diesel" Hornezes

CHRISTOPHER "DIESEL" HORNEZES

First Edition 2025

Printed in the United States of America

This is a work of fiction. Names, characters, places, and incidents either are products of the author's imagination or are used fictitiously. Any similarity to actual events or locales or persons, living or dead, is entirely coincidental.

Lock Down Publications
P.O. Box 944
Stockbridge, GA 30281
www.lockdownpublications.com

Like our page on Facebook: Lock Down Publications
www.facebook.com/lockdownpublications.ldp

By: Christopher A. Hornezes #704976
Racine Correctional Institution
P.O. Box 189
Phoenix, MD 21131

Stay Connected with Us!

Text **LOCKDOWN** to 22828 to stay up-to-date with new releases, sneak peaks, contests and more…

Like our page on Facebook:
Lock Down Publications

Join Lock Down Publications/The New Era Reading Group

Visit our website:
www.lockdownpublications.com

Follow us on Instagram:
Lock Down Publications

Email Us: We want to hear from you!

Chapter 1

Bunz was so shocked that her knees grew weak. She fell backwards against the Over Finch edition Range Rover, bowing her head, shaking it, unwilling to believe that Eric was really in front of her. Sonya's jaw was nearly on the ground as her childhood play-brother walked to the woman he had made believe he was dead for an entire year.

"No…no…no, no, no, noooo! This isn't real! He's not here!" Bunz told herself.

"Monique."

She swore she heard his voice. She refused to look up. She felt a hand take hers.

"Mo-Mo," she heard him said. "Baby. Look at me."

Bunz opened her watery eyes and raised her head.

She looked into his deep brown eyes. They were full of liquid, love and compassion. They made her nearly swoon over the thuggishly handsome ghost.

"How are you here?" she asked, her voice breaking up from her emotions going haywire.

"It's a looong story," Eric told her, "but I'm here. I never left, to keep it a hunnid."

He looked at his Persian's play-sister. Her eyes were still wide with shock, filled with tears, with a hand over her mouth. "Sis." Eric stepped up to her. "I know you're very—"

SMACK!

His words were stopped by her open hand, flying into his face. He knew it was coming, but thought the mother of his twin babies would've beat Sonya to it.

"Asshole! What the fuck, Eric!" Sonya cried, so angry that she wanted to smack him twice more.

"I had to play dead, Sonya. I needed that bitch to think Bunz was unprotected so I could get her ass once and for all."

"You abandoned us," Bunz interjected, standing upright and glaring at him.

"I was close by the whole time, baby," he told her, turning back to her.

SMACK!

Bunz fired his ass up without even a second thought. Eric took it like a man. He looked at her and saw so much hurt in her eyes. It made his own heart hurt.

"Mo-Mo, I'm—"

SMACK!

Sonya's hand went across his face again.

"Come on yo, why y'all gotta—"

SMACK!

Bunz lit him up again.

"Okay, y'all asses are really trippin'," he told them, backing away before another one came.

"You played dead...for five months! Your son and daughter have never seen anything but a fucking picture!" Bunz snapped. She burst into tears then. She didn't know whether to be furious or happy as a pig in mud that the love of her life wasn't dead.

Risking another open hand, Eric stepped back up to his future wife. He was able to take her hands into his. She allowed him to hold onto them. Eric was beyond happy to see that she was still wearing the 8-carat diamond engagement ring he had put on her finger at McArthur's down in Chicago.

"Mo-Mo," he said to her, soft and gentle.

She looked up at him.

"I'm sorry, baby. Tell me what I can do to be forgiven."

Bunz sniffled and said, "Slap yourself."

"Hard!" added Sonya, wiping tears from her face.

"Why y'all gotta be so violent?"

"You're the hitman," Bunz reminded him.

Eric chuckled. "Any chance I can meet my babies and see my dogs?"

Bunz smiled. "Yes. We live up in Caledonia."

"I know where you live, Monique."

"You could've, you know, like stopped by and said hello, goddammit."

He shook his head. "Three weeks."

Bunz and Sonya both furrowed their eyebrows.

"Three weeks...what?" Sonya asked.

"The time it's gon' take for me to get out of the dog house," he surmised.

"Ha!" Bunz laughed. "You might wanna go by yourself some fluffy blankets for all the nights you'll be on that couch, player. Don't think I forgot what else you did."

Eric furrowed his brows. "Something worse than playin' dead for so long?"

"Yeah, nigga! You fucked that bitch!" Bunz snapped.

Sonya gasped. "Eric!"

"Uh...I can explain that."

SMACK!

"BUNZ! STOP SMACKIN'—"

SMACK!

"SONYA!"

"ERIC!" Sonya yelled back

"I swear to God, y'all are really crazy, joe. We got other things we could be doin' instead of smackin' me. Andrea is in the wrong hands, and we're standin' here where she got snatched up."

Bunz sighed. "You're right. That little bitch is nuts."

"We will get her back," Sonya declared, pulling her iPhone out of her hand bag. "And when I catch that honkie bitch, I'ma put her face through a glass windshield for fucking my Range Rover up."

Bunz and Eric stood at Sonya's side as she made a call. Seconds later, she started speaking.

"I want any and everything owned by Paula Paulmatti and her associates sent to me right now," they heard her say before she ended the call. She then looked at them both. "Playtime is over; Paula Paulmatti is gonna beg to die when I get my hands on her."

***

She couldn't see anything, but she could hear and feel that she was in a vehicle. Her hands were behind her back, wrists tied, ankles bound. Fear of the unknown had set in. Andrea was terrified. She heard what Paula said to whom she assumed was Bunz, and or Sonya. There was no mention of a trade or how she was going to be freed. Paula Paulmatti was going to torture and kill her, then she was going to get Bunz.

The ride seemed to be never-ending. Her body hurt; the restraints were digging into her flesh. After what felt like hours, the vehicle finally came to a stop, and the engine shut off. Less than a minute later, she heard the sound of a sliding door opening up. A pair of hands grabbed her feet.

Andrea shrieked and kicked hard.

"AHH! YOU BITCH!" she heard after her high-heeled feet hit what felt like a face.

CRACK!

A fist flew into her face dazing her.

"Do that again, you stupid whore, and I'm gonna shove my cock up your ass before you die!" she heard the man threaten.

"Fuck you, bitch!" Andrea snapped back.

The hands grabbed her and yanked her out of the vehicle. Andrea felt herself hit the ground.

"Cut her face and take the bag off of her head."

Andrea recognized the female's voice that spoke right away. Andrea's restraints were cut away. The bag was removed from her head. She saw she was in the woods. A small log cabin was a few yards away. Surrounding her were four big dudes. Two stepped to the side and revealed the little petitely built Italian chick.

Andrea sneered as Paula stepped forward, strutting her stuff like a stuck-up runway model in her Valentino bodysuit, with matching stilettos, and her long hair hanging loosely down her shoulders. She stepped right up to Andrea, slightly dwarfed by her.

"So. You are my long, lost sister, huh?" Paula asked.

CRACK!

Andrea head-butted her square in the face breaking her nose. Paula screamed in pain, nose gushing blood.

"BITCH!" she screamed, jumping back.

"GET THE FUCK OFF OF ME, PUSSY!"

Andrea screamed trying to wiggle from under him.

Paula's feet appeared by her face.

WHAM!

A stiletto rocked Andrea's jaw, dazing her. Paula kicked her again, then again, then once more.

"Stupid bitch. You think it's a game! Let's play then! GET HER UP AND IN THE BASEMENT! NOOOOW!"

Andrea was grabbed up and forced into the house. The bag was put back over her head as she was carried down the stairs. Her eyes filled with tears, as she was taken to where she knew she would never leave from alive.

"I love you, Tim. Please don't forget me, baby," she thought to herself as his face appeared in her mind; the only man she had ever developed true feeling for, that she was never going to be able to see again…

Chapter 2

The chauffeured executive-edition Cadillac Escalade ESU turned into the driveway of the lavish mini-mansion, out in Caledonia, Wisconsin. The driver pulled up to the front door and parked. Eric parked his crotch-rocket next to it. The door flew open as Bunz got out. Eric saw his younger cousin in the doorway with a look of shock on her face. Tracy ran to him, tears falling from her eyes as she lost all control of her emotions.

"Eric! Oh my God!" she cried in his arms, squeezing him tightly. "You're alive! You're really alive!"

Seconds later, Deuce and LaLa, Eric's two big bulky brown brindle XXL Bullies, ran out of the house, overjoyed for the return of the man that had raised and trained them.

"How though, E?" asked Tracy, voice breaking. "How are you alive?"

Eric kissed his younger cousin's forehead, then hugging her tightly in his muscular arms, told her, "I been a killer for a long time. Sometimes, I wear body armor and don't even realize it, 'til I get shot by a crazy-ass bitch that thinks shits sweet. But nonetheless, I'm back, and I'll never leave y'all like that again."

Tracy pulled back and wiped the tears from her eyes.

"E?" she said to him.

"Yeah," he replied.

SMACK!

Bunz busted out laughing.

9

Eric turned to her. "How many more times am I gon' get slapped before I get to hold my babies?"

She shrugged. "Depends."

He shook his head at her, then went to shower his tiger-striped killers with some love. Bunz then led them into her home. Eric looked around and nodded in approval. Bunz took his hand and led him and Tracy to where Eric Jr. and Monique were laid out on Bunz's big bed, in her massive master bedroom. His eyes begin welling up with tears as he laid them on the miniature versions of him and Bunz. His almost 11 month old son and daughter were both wide awake, their little hands and arms and legs flailing and kicking.

Eric walked up to the bed. Bunz, Tracy and the dogs stayed where they were and watched as he looked down at them. They heard Eric Jr. giggle as he looked up at his father. Monique's legs kicked faster, then she started to giggle.

"Hey, little ones," Eric said in a soft voice, sitting on the bed with them. "It's nice to finally meet y'all. I'm yo' daddy."

Bunz watched her fiancé pick Eric Jr. up with his right arm, then Monique with his left. He looked at the two, awestruck that they had come from him and her. He kissed his son's face, then turned to kiss Monique's when her hand came out and lightly popped his cheek. Bunz and Tracy started laughing.

"Guess you had it comin' from her, too." Bunz chuckled.

She and Tracy took flicks of him holding his babies for the first time. The moment was captured and saved to be viewed forever.

Eric looked at his woman a second later. "Bae. Tomorrow, there's some people we need to go meet. They have some things they need help with."

"Some people?" Bunz asked with puzzled eyebrows.

"Yup. Don't worry. You will definitely like them."

"I need sleep. I still can't even think straight," Tracy said. She walked up to Eric, hugged him tightly, then Bunz. She kissed the twins and left out. Eric Jr. and his younger sister by a few hours both yawned.

"They're tired," Eric said with a warm smile.

"Lemme put 'em down for a nap," Bunz said. She gently took them from Eric and took them to their crib in the next room. Leaning in, she kissed them on their cheeks. Bunz returned and saw Deuce and LaLa sitting in front of her fiancé. Their tails wagged as he gave them ear rubs. She smiled knowing the two beasts would probably never willingly let Eric out of their sight again. "Eric?"

He looked up from her. She was so beautiful that looking at her was like looking at Black Perfection. She was both sexy and classy in the green Dolce & Gabbana skirt suit, with a silky white blouse under the jacket, brown pantyhose, and gold pumps that had 6-inch heels and pointed toes. Her long gold dreads were wrapped up and styled in a ball on the top of her head. Her makeup was minimal. Matching her shiny stilettos. Gold Cartiers framed her beautiful face.

Eric remembered when he first met the caramel complexion Jamaican, Puerto Rican and Cambodian stallion. It was at a nightclub down in Chicago where she had been a dancer. She had his eyes the minute he saw her, and he had hers. Bunz was entranced by her thuggishly handsome fiancé. His peanut butter skin, his body builder size. 6'1" frame, his long hair that was three shades of brown, with a razor sharp beard. His facial structure was strong, well-pronounce. He looked bigger to Bunz from when she last saw him on that horrible day that she thought Paula had taken him out.

"Talk to me beautiful," he said standing up as she walked up to him. "And please, Monique, please don't smack me."

She laughed. "Naw. I'm not gonna smack you, baby. What I am gonna do is punish you in a whole other way."

"Oh yeah?" he asked, his eyes lighting up like they were wired to a big battery. Eric wrapped his arms around her waist and pulled her to him. "How you gon' do that?"

"It's your fault that this pussy hasn't gotten worked out in so long." Bunz made him lean his head down and planted a kiss on his lips. "So, since you're back to me..." She kissed him again as his hands slid down and cupped her phat round 48-inch ass. "You are gonna make up for five, long, loveless nights; all in one day, sir."

Eric kissed her then, sticking his tongue into her mouth. He tongued her down, backing her up to one of her dressers and as her plump rear bumped it, he worked her skirt up over her hips. Bunz grew so hot from the feeling of his hands, lips, and tongue. Half of her thought it was all just a dream, but even dreams didn't have her pussy as wet as it was at that moment. Her thong and pantyhose were soaked.

She reached down and worked his shirt up as Eric ripped the crotch of her stockings. His shirt came off, and his toned muscular upper body was revealed. As he lifted her up, Bunz saw the scars on his chest and his defined abs. She knew they were made by Paula when she shot him. Eric sat her up on the dresser. He reached in, grabbed her thong, and yanked, snatching it off, uncovering her swollen southern lips. He licked his lips at her dripping wet center, then lowered his head to smell what he had been missing for waay too damn long.

Bunz felt as giddy as a young school girl on her Sweet 16, being led out to where her new car sat, purchased by her parents. Her former life in prostitution and exotic dancing had brought about many guys and girls, but not a single person that she had given some pussy or ass to had ever gotten her as hot as Eric did and does. He was her Papoose, and she was his Remy Ma. Black love in the rawest form that could not be broken.

Bunz reached up, clapped her hands, activating the studio-quality audio system built into her room. Jhene Aiko's

"SATIVA," featuring Rae Sremmurd, started playing a second later. Eric opened her legs up wide, parting her thick thighs. He kissed them, licking them through the soaked fabric of her ripped pantyhose. Bunz bit her bottom lip, back arching, a moan escaping her, as his kisses moved close to her throbbing box.

At her womanhood, Eric ran his tongue up her slit, lapping her juices up like a kitten lapping up milk. He relished her sweet taste, remembering how she always tasted so fresh and clean, even after a long day. He peeled her open and put his lips to her enlarged clitoris. Bunz moaned out as he started sucking on it, swirling his tongue around it, pleasing her so much that her toes curled up in her pumps.

"Eric! Yes!" she cried out as he dined on her. "Shit, baby! God, I missed you!"

He ate her up like she was his favorite meal. He worked her, making her head spin around and around. He made her body respond in ways only he knew how to do.

Khalid's *"OTW"* with Black and Ty Dolla $ign came on as Eric inserted two fingers inside of her. He continued dining on her while he finger-fucked her tight tunnel. He aimed to make her yearn for penetration. Bunz ran her hands over his cornrows as she felt herself getting close to climaxing. The sensational pleasures he was so great at giving her always got her there. She cried out his name a minute later, right before she exploded, squirting in his face.

Bunz nearly collapsed. She hadn't had an orgasm in months. Hell, she'd damn near lost her sex drive, but now, she had her mojo back and had no intentions of allowing anything less than five rounds.

"Fuck!" she cursed, feeling like she had no air in her lungs.

Eric licked her clean, then stood. Without words, he relieved his woman of her suit jacket, her blouse, and her bra. He freed her succulent 36DD breasts and sucked on them, getting her even hotter. He kicked his Jordans off, dropped his 501's and boxers— ten inches of hard dick throbbing, pointing right at what it wanted. Bunz licked her lips at the sight of his pipe. She wanted to suck on it until he nutted down her throat, but right as she went to jump down to fall to her knees and put it in her mouth, Eric halted her.

"Naw, baby. This is all me. Lemme show you how sorry I am that I left you and my kids. You can suck on this dick another day, but right now, I'm finna beat this pussy up real good," he told her.

Bunz's eyes rolled to the back of her head when she felt him slide inside of her. He stretched her walls out. It stung but felt so good. Everything about his love came rushing back to her, making it mean so much more. Eric put it on her on the dresser. He took her down on the floor, then they ended up on the bed. They went strong, round after round after round, going until they both ran out of gas. They climaxed together, their sixth time. Fatigue, exhaustion; both set in. They passed out, sweaty and hot, intertwined with each other, hearts beating as one. Eric had his woman back. Bunz had her man back. Now, they needed Andrea back, and neither planned to let anyone associated with Paula Paulmatti live for what the little bitch had done.

***

Around 8 o'clock that evening, Bunz, Eric, the twins, and the dogs were out in the backyard sitting on a big blanket that was spread out over a large section of grass. Eric held their daughter while Bunz held their son. LaLa laid her head on Deuce's stomach while they both watched. The two enjoyed their first real day as a family. Bunz got emotional a few times as it all set in that Eric was really back. Her iPhone rang while Eric Jr. giggled at her goofy faces. Eric saw Tim's name on her screen and looked at her as she answered.

"Tim," Bunz said, putting it on speaker.

"That's how you get down, fam? You let my girl get snatched up after you drop a bomb-shell on her, and then you ain't even tryna go look for her!"

"Whoa. Tim, relax, she's—"

"NO! I'M NOT RELAXED! HOW THE FUCK CAN YOU EVEN TELL ME THAT, BUNZ? THAT BITCH HAS MY GIRL!" Tim yelled angrily.

Eric spoke up, not liking how his former dope runner was talking to his lady. "Aye, Tim," he said.

There was a silence on Tim's end for nearly a minute. "Man, who the fuck is that?" Tim asked. "Aye, Bunz! What the fuck, joe? My big homie gone 'n you move on that fast?"

Bunz gasped and went to snap on who'd been like a little brother to her in Eric's absence.

Eric stopped her. "Tim, I'ma need you to get off the gas pedal and breathe, bruh."

Silence again. Bunz hadn't told Tim that Eric was alive. When he found out, she knew for a fact that he was going to go ape shit.

"Naw, man...hell no!" Tim said. "Bunz! Who is that, fam?"

"It's me, Tim. Eric."

"Maan, no it's not! I was at his funeral! My boy is dead! Keep playin' wit' me and I'ma rock yo' muhfuckin' ass to sleep, fam! On God!"

"Tim, where are you?" Bunz asked.

"Home! Tryin' to keep from blowin' my brains out, but what the fuck is the point of life without my girl!"

"Tim! Come on, naw man! You're tweakin' real hard right now!" Bunz snapped which startled Eric Jr, causing him to cry. "Dammit! Tim! Stay home! I'm on my way!" she told him. Bunz sat herself upright and cradled her baby so she could get up.

"Bae. Stay here," Eric told her. "I'll go."

"Eric, he's not thinkin' right."

15

Eric laid his daughter on the blanket and got up. "I know. I got him, baby," Eric told her. "I'll be back. LaLa! Come!"

Bunz watched the female Bully hop up to follow him. "E?" she called out to him, reaching for her son while Deuce stood up.

He turned back to her.

"I love you, baby," Bunz told him.

"I love you too, my queen. I will be back," he told her, then walked off with LaLa in tow.

Chapter 3

"Fuck this shit, joe! Bitchass shit! I gotta get my girl back!" Tim declared, grabbing the loaded AK-47 from off the bed next to him. "People got me all the way fucked up, joe! I'm finna kill e'rybody!"

He grabbed the keys to his Mercedes SLR McLaren and dipped out of his lavish home with murder on his mind. Tim floored the half-million dollar car. The super-charged V8 engine roared out of the pipes that stuck out from under the car, right behind the front wheels. He sped recklessly down I-94 from Oakcreek, all the way down to Racine and hopped on Highway 20. He flew down 20 until he came to the big parking lot where the new Italian restaurant sat by itself. The lot was nearly jam packed with vehicles. Inside, many people waited for a table. The Mediterranean cuisine served there was reported to be to die for. Tim was about to make that a true statement.

***

"Marvelous! Absolutely delicious, Marco! This is the best fettuccine I have ever tasted that isn't made by my mother!"

17

said Donnie Paulmatti, a heavy-set man, balding up top, clean shaven face, wearing a custom tailored Brioni suit.

With him was his equally heavy wife Angela— a brown-haired woman with an annoying sense of entitlement. "I wouldn't say all that," she told the restaurant's manager. "The pasta feels a little too much like dough to me, Marco."

Donnie looked at his wife. "Why you gotta be such a sourpuss, Angie?"

"Don't you talk to me like that, Donovan! I am your wife!" she shot back.

Not for long, you boring cunt, he thought to himself, so ready to divorce her and get with the hot, young Sicilian chick he'd been fucking behind his wife's back. "Sorry, dear," he said instead, not wanting to argue.

Mario stayed quiet until he was brought back into the conversation.

"How's the lasagna here?" Donnie asked just as a waiter came with a bottle of white wine to refill their glasses.

"To die for," Mario told him. "I use the best cheese and sauce with sausage and beef brought in from Venice. My chi—"

BRRRRRRR! BRRRRRRRR!

Gun shots rang out before he could finish his sentence. People in the restaurant screamed as bullets blew through the tall floor-to-ceiling glass windows, hitting everyone in their path.

"SHIT!" Donnie cursed.

He pulled his 9-millimeter Beretta from inside his suit jacket. Angela got her own from her Gucci hand bag. Mario ran, terrified as he watched bodies drop and body parts fly.

Donnie and his wife saw the shooter outside of their niece's restaurant, dumping a semi-automatic assault rifle at anyone moving with no regard to human life. "Son of a bitch! Fucking nigger has the balls to pull this shit!" Donnie snapped.

18

He and Angela started firing at him, gripping their pistols with both hands, aiming for his head.

***

Tim hopped out of his Benz with his chopper and walked right up to the front of the restaurant. He looked at all the people inside, eating drinking, laughing, having a great time. He raised the barrel of his AK-47 at the long and tall window. A woman happened to turn and look at him. She went to scream right before he squeezed the trigger.

Gritting his teeth, Tim sprayed at everyone. He gave no fucks who he hit. He swept left, right, back to left and right. He sent swarms of 7.62-millimeter rounds flying, attacking like angry African killer bees. Heads exploded like balloons filled with blood and meat. Chests opened up like mini explosions went off inside. He blew down so many people faster than a professional bowler hit a strike. He left off of the trigger, dumped the extended clip out, slapped in a fresh one, and made his move advancing on the eatery to kill everyone inside.

BOC! BOC! BOC! BOC! BOC! BOC! BOC! BOC! BOC! BOC! BOC! BOC! BOC! BOC!

"AAHH! FUUUCK!" Tim howled as a bullet slammed into his chest. "GODDAMN, THAT HURT!" He was glad that he'd had the sense to slap on his bullet-proof vest before he even got his AK-47 out. Even more furious, Tim saw where the gunshots were coming from. He saw a fat man and a fat woman popping at him with pistols from by a table surrounded by dead bodies. "WOOOOOO! Y'ALL WANNA PLAY! LET'S GOOOOOO!" Tim screamed maniacally, then pulled the trigger as he ran towards the restaurant.

"Holy hell!" Donnie said in shock as he hit the shooter, right in the chest, but the man didn't fall. "Son of a bitch!"

"HE'S GOT ARMOR ON, DON!" Angela shouted.

BRRRRRRRR! BRRRRRRRR! BRRRRR!
The man blew at them wildly. Angela caught one in her chest, then Donnie turned to her, blood, brains, and pieces of skull smacked him in his face as a slug exploded her head.

"Well...guess a divorce isn't needed now," he said to himself, then chuckled.

More shots came in his direction. He saw the shooter stepping through where the window used to be. Donnie raised his gun and pulled the trigger.

CLICK, CLICK, CLICK, CLICK

"SHIT!" he panicked, realizing he was empty. He looked at the man. He was close enough to see the diabolical grin on his face.

"BA-DA-DA-DA-DAA! DIE, FAT ASS!" the guy sang, raising his AK up and pointing it at Donnie.

Right as he wrapped his finger around the trigger... a massive dog ran in and jumped on Donnie, taking him down to the blood soaked floor.

"AAAHHH! GET OFF! GET OFF! GET OOOOOF!" Donnie cried as the huge tiger-striped Bully's sharp teeth champed into the side of his face.

Tim knew LaLa anywhere. He looked at her with pure shock as she ripped his cheek off and ate it.

"What the hell?" he asked himself as the fat Italian screamed in agony.

"That's what I said when I heard the way yo' ass was talkin' to my woman."

Tim spun around and pointed his chopper at the individual that stood about 6 feet away from him. His jaw dropped. His eyes went wide. He was rendered speechless.

"LALA! COME!" yelled Eric.

The dog obeyed, hopping off of the crying man, running to her human's side with blood smeared all over her snout.

"N-N-Naw...how the fuck? E?"

Eric grinned and nodded. "Yup. You and I gon' have to talk about how you speak to women, but for now, let's grab dude and get up outta here."

Tim, still somewhat in shock, nodded his head. He ran to where the overweight man writhed in pain, his exposed jawbone and teeth a gruesome sight. Tim went to grab him, but the guy snatched away.

CRACK!

Tim fired his jaw up, sleeping him, making it easier to drag him out. He turned, wondering if Eric was really there, or did he die and get sucked into some alternate universe.

Eric stood where he'd been. LaLa stood next to him, panting with her tongue hanging out of her mouth. "Fuck is you waitin' for lil nigga?" Eric asked, then tapped the dial of his G-shock watch. "Time is not on our side! Hurry up!"

"This nigga heavy as hell, fam! I need help!"

"You ain't think of that when yo' wild ass came chargin' over here in a $500,000 Benz, nigga! Knock it the fuck off and use them muscles! Hurry up before the cops come!"

Tim managed to drag the fat Italian out of the restaurant. Eric made him drag the guy to where his plain-looking windowless Chevy van was parked a couple rows over. Muscling the Italian inside, Eric took over, tying his wrists, ankles, gagging him, and blindfolding him. Tim ran to his Benz and jumped in, amazed that he still didn't hear any sirens. He push-started the engine and peeled off to catch up with Eric, still stuck in disbelief that the man he swore was gone, the man that took him from being a mediocre pee-on in the streets to a boss dope man, and a fearless killer, was back in the flesh.

***

"You finished?" the Commander of the Racine Police Department asked, answering Eric's call.

"Take it away, my man. Problem solved; thank you for your services," Eric replied and ended the call.

In the back of his torture van, Eric heard the man waking up. Frantic movements and groaning came. The guy started screaming for help a second later. Sitting at his side, LaLa started growling at him, the hairs on her back standing up as she grew angrier. Eric grabbed the taser from the cupholder, turned his hand back and fired.

"AAAAAAHHHHH YAYAYAAAA!" The Italian screamed as Eric fried him.

Seconds later, the screaming stopped. Eric let off the trigger, then let the taser rest in the pocket in the side of the seat. He reached out to the volume knob on the dash and turned the music up, blasting Fabolous and Jadakiss' *"SOUL FOOD"*. He rapped along with Jadakiss' verse, leading Tim out to where the torture dome, as he called it, awaited to be utilized to handle the business, and get Paula Paulmatti's attention.

***

Bunz laughed as she heard her future husband rapping out loud. On the screen of her iPhone, she could see him via video call in his torture van. Eric looked at her and winked, giving her the prize winning smile that had her at hello nearly 3 and a half years prior.

"Bae, yo' ass crazy," she told him.

"Tim's crazier. This nigga got to singin' that McDonald's theme when he was about to blow fat ass down. Nigga said *'BA-DA-DA-DA-DAAA!'*"

Bunz laughed her ass off. "Yeah. He does that for some reason. At least he's still somewhat himself, but he won't be Tim until Andrea's back. E, he really loves her, baby."

"Any man that'll blow a whole mob-affiliated restaurant down on behalf of a chick, I would be inclined to agree." They continued talking for another half an hour until Eric reached his torture dome. "Lemme see if I can make him sing like Frank Sinatra. Love you, beautiful."

"Love you too, handsome."

***

"FUCK YOU!" Donnie shouted out at the two.

SMACK!

A big leather belt with metal rivets in it left another bloody welt across his large stomach. Held up by wrist restraints, he dangled from the contraption that was meant for leather hides to hang from while being tanned. His body was covered in welts, scrapes, burns and cuts. His right eye was swollen shut, and his nose completely gone, inside of LaLa's stomach.

"You's a real tough guy. I'll give you that, my dude."

Donnie looked down at the two light brown skinned men. One had long braids, the other a messy fade, blue eyes and a rough looking beard. He looked like he'd been through hell and back.

"Fuck you!" he said again.

POW!

"AAAAAAAGGHHHH-FUUUUUUCK!"   Donnie screamed as a 6-inch copper nail shot through his knee cap.

The blue-eyed man held the powerful nail gun, powered by cartridges filled with gun powder. The braided man dropped the belt and went to the steel table topped with so many instruments of torture that even the devil would cringe at what they could do.

"You think that hurts?" the man said picking up a plastic looking gun. "Wait 'til you feel how much a tattoo removal gun hurts when I put it to your only other eye, bitch."

"Aye, E. Hold up a sec. What about dude's phone?" Donnie heard Blue Eyes say to Braids.

"What about it?"

"This that bitch's uncle, right? Bet money her number in his jack. We call her and negotiate a trade for Drea."

Donnie saw Braids nod.

"Never hurts to try. Go for it, player."

Tim got the Italian's phone out of the pocket of his pants. There was no security lock on it, so he was able to go right into the contacts. "Bingo. Let's give Miss Paulmatti a call, or how about a video call so she can see that her uncle's life is on the line." Tim video called Paula.

As it rang, Eric stroked behind LaLa's ears, praising her for a job well-done. The Italian was in so much pain and had lost so much blood that he was fading out.

The video was answered in four rings. Paula's face appeared on the screen. The second she saw Tim's face, her eyebrows furrowed. "What the fuck! You're that blue-eyed bitch from the club in Racine!" she remembered as the night her boyfriend Rubio lost the top of his head by a machete.

Hearing her voice, Eric stepped over to Tim and shared his face. "And I'm the nigga that made yo' boyfriend lose his head," he told her, "and the guy you sucked off and thought you killed."

Seeing Paula's shocked face, Tim asked, "Where is my girl?"

She started smirking then. "She's down in the basement; my big cousins are running trains on that whore."

Tim nearly exploded. Eric put a hand on his shoulder, stopping Tim's well-known anger.

"Check it out, Paula," said Eric. "You have somethin' that we want, and we have somethin' that you want. Care to do a little tradin'?"

"You got my diamonds?" she asked Eric.

"I have somethin' more precious than rocks, lil mama." He switched the camera view so that the video call displayed Paula's uncle. He and Tim could still see her face in the little square in the corner of the screen. They saw her reaction and it was priceless.

"What did you do to him?" she asked, looking at her battered family member.

"We fucked his fat ass up, bitch! Yo auntie is—"

"In the living room tied up," Eric interjected, cutting Tim off so as to keep Paula from knowing her aunt was already dead.

"He's still alive. Give us Andrea, we'll give you yo' uncle."

Paula looked at Eric and Tim for almost a minute. The silence between them felt like it was the loudest subwoofers made. Then suddenly, she busted out laughing. Eric and Tim both furrowed as the girl laughed hysterically.

"Care to share what's so funny?" Eric asked.

"You!" Paula told him, laughing so hard that her eyes filled with tears. "And your punk bitch blue-eyed home boy! I do not give a mother-fuck about that fat, bloody slob of meat! Nor do I give a fuck about his whore wife, whom, by the way is laid out without a head, not in your living room. You think I haven't found out about my restaurant? Just like you've got cops in your pocket, so do I. You can keep him. I'm keeping your bitch, Blue Eyes, and only after my cousins wear her pussy and asshole out, will I kill the bitch and hack her into pieces that'll end up feeding a few poor, starving kids. Buh-bye now, bitches!"

The screen went blank then.

"Damn…that's is a cold bitch," Eric said shaking his head.

Tim saw red. He raised the nail gun up, pointing it at the Italian's face.

Weakly the man looked at him with barely open eyes. He saw the nail gun pointing at him. "F-F-Fuck you…nigger," he managed to say.

"Fuck yo' momma, bitch!" Tim shot back.

PACK! PACK! PACK! PACK! PACK! PACK! PACK!

Tim emptied the whole 20 nail clip, making the Italian look like the Hellraiser. Blood leaked, spilling down onto the floor. The Italian's body swung slightly as if a light gust of wind blew against it.

Eric patted Tim's back. "Good job, lil homie. I'll take it from her," he told him.

Infuriated, Tim stepped back and let his big homie step in. He watched Eric go and pick up a large device that looked like a leaf blower. Eric put the straps on his shoulders like a book bag. He walked over to the dead man, raised the plastic hose's sprout at him then pressed the button.

Tim was thinking flames were going to shoot out and cook the Italian, but instead of fire, clear liquid sprayed out. Eric pretended like he was hosing down a car. He whistled a pleasant tune as he doused the fat man. 15 seconds later, he stopped spraying and stepped back. Tim's eyes widened when he saw the man literally begin to melt before his very eyes. Chunks of flesh dropped and splattered on the floor. Bone broke away and fizzled. Eric watched his special blend of industrial acids eat away the Italian until he was a puddle of gelatin on the ground.

Eric put the acid blaster away, got the hose and washed the remains down a drain. Before he was done he sprayed a high strength cleaner on the ground that made even the most sophisticated forensic tests unable to detect any DNA or blood.

Tim chuckled. "Man, E. It's good to have you back, fam. Niggas missed you, bruh."

"Good to be back, Timmy Tim Tim," Eric replied putting everything up so they could go.

"Just do me a favor."

"You already know. Talk to me, big homie."

Eric looked at him. "No more blowin' down mob restaurants after hoppin' out a half-million dollar Mercedes-Benz."

"Says the guy that pulls drive-bys in a Bentley 'n shit." Tim laughed as Eric shook his head and laughed himself.

Chapter 4

The following morning, Eric awoke to the feeling of a warm wetness around his cock. He opened his eyes to see his woman hunched over next to him on her knees, swallowing his 10-inch pipe.

Bunz saw he had woken up. She took his dick out of her mouth, smiled at him. "Good morning, my King. Today is going to be a great day. I am going to please you every chance I get," she told him, then took his dick back into her mouth, taking it all the way to the back of her throat.

Eric's eyes rolled to the back of his head. His toes curled up. He groaned and cursed as his future wife gave him the best dome ever. Bunz gripped him at the base and deep-throated him like a certified dick sucking pro. Hearing her man groan, seeing how he could not lay still because of how good she was giving head had her pussy soaking wet. Pleasing him had her so horny.

She released his cock from her mouth again and spat on it. She gripped it with a hand and started jerking it while talking dirty to him. Eric's body arched up off the bed as he came close to cumming. Bunz stopped suddenly, feeling his

27

dick pulsating in her hand. She climbed on top of him, a knee on each side of his body. Eric looked up at the beautiful caramel stallion as she slid her wetness over his hardness. She looked down into his eyes and started riding him. She leaned down and kissed his lips.

She made love to her man. She treated him like her king, then Eric took over and treated her like his queen. He loved her from behind, infatuated by how phat her ass was and how it jiggled when his thighs smacked against it every time he went in. Bunz reached back, grabbing her meaty booty cheeks as she laid her face on the bed. She opened herself up. Eric leaned down and ran his tongue up her crack. She squealed in delight from the feeling of his tongue swirling around her puckered asshole. Eric spit on it, making sure it was wet enough for him to slide right in. He raised up and smacked her asshole with his throbbing cock, demanding that she tell him to put it in her ass. Like a good freak, Bunz obeyed, pleading for him to dominate her.

He eased the bulbous tip in and gently pushed inside. Bunz gritted her teeth as the way he stretched her tight anal tract stung but felt so good to her. She relished in the pleasureful sensation, loving how dirty and sexy his dick in her ass made her feel. He treated her like his lady but fucked her like a thot. Bunz would have it no other way, and neither would he.

Eric's nut came seconds later after Bunz exploded for the third time. He pulled his dick out and blew his hot globs all over her asshole, coating it completely. He plopped down next to her, spent of energy. Bunz laid on her side, cuddling up with him. He pulled her body to his and held her.

"I love you, E," Bunz said with misty eyes.

Eric smiled. He planted a kiss on her forehead and reciprocated her words, spitting them from the bottom of his heart. His alarm went off a minute later. He reached over to where his phone was on the nightstand and grabbed it. "Time to get up and get at it, love" Eric told her. "Tracy should be here any minute."

Bunz nodded. "Problem solving day, huh?"

"Yep. Solvin' some big problems and securing our future, and our son's and daughter's futures."

***

After they showered, Bunz breastfed their babies while Eric got dressed, rocking a black Prada t-shirt, black jeans, and leather Prada sneakers. He took over while Bunz went to get dressed. He grabbed raw steaks from the fridge and fed the dogs, watching them tear the big slabs up like Chico, the Bull Terrier on the movie *Next Friday.*

Eric Jr. and his sister both giggled at the big dogs, finding it hilarious how they ate. Tracy entered the kitchen just then. She was dressed in a black, brown and tan Gucci top and skirt outfit, with high-toped Red Bottom sneakers matching. She wore no make-up at all and rocked her hair in a big puffy afro. Her natural beauty was radiant and made her stand out like a true black queen always did. She hugged her big cousin emphatically, holding on to him for a good minute. She was still so happy that he was back. After she let him go, Tracy went and planted kisses all over the twins' faces.

Lala and Deuce finished inhaling their food and trotted up to Tracy, tails wagging as the scent of Tracy's own killer Pit Bull filled their noses.

"So, how is Tim doin', cuzzo?" Tracy asked Eric as she patted LaLa's and Deuce's heads.

"His ass goin' crazy," Eric replied as LaLa went up to him and nudged his side with her nose.

"He really love that girl. I hope to God that we can get her back, or else that nigga will kill the muthafuckin' world."

Fully understanding what her cousin was telling her, Tracy nodded her head. She already knew how Tim got

29

down. She felt sorry for Paula Paulmatti whenever Tim got his hands on her…almost.

A minute later, Bunz entered the kitchen and Eric's jaw dropped to the floor.

"Well damn, girl! That's what chu on?" Tracy asked, looking at Bunz like she had never seen Bunz get dolled up until now.

Bunz smiled flirtatiously at her man. The skin-tight and ultra bright white bodysuit clung to her amazingly curvaceous body like it was a second skin. Her long golden locks hung loosely down her shoulders with a dark-blue and white bucket hat on her head that had Dior monogrammed all over it. Down on her feet were matching monogrammed Dior high tops that resembled a pair of Chuck Taylors

Hanging around her neck were two long white-gold and diamond chains. Both of them flicked like the diamond-encrusted Cartier on her wrist. Her lips glossed from the dark-blue lipstick matching her eyelids, and as she stepped in, the kitchen began to smell like fresh tropical fruit.

"Wow, wow, wow, wooow! Shit!" Eric went up to his fiancée, pulled her to him, wrapped her up in his arms, and kissed her like he would never see her again.

"Get a room, horn-ball muthafuckas," Tracy joked, making her way back over to the little ones.

Bunz felt her temperature rising the more they lip-boxed. His hands slid down to her phat ass and gave her cheeks a squeeze. His dick got as hard as a steel pipe from how good her body felt against his. Bunz felt his manhood poking her. It had her starting to grow moist between her legs. She quickly pulled back before she soaked herself.

"Stop tryna make me catch a fire, Eric," she told him, feeling like she needed to take a dive into the freezer for a few minutes.

"Stop lookin' so good then," Eric replied, hands still gripping her juicy rearend.

"I can't. I woke up like this."

Eric and Tracy laughed their asses off at Bunz.

"Maan, it's good to be back," Eric said then, and stole one more kiss from his flawlessly beautiful example of black perfection in the flesh.

***

Eric and Bunz kissed their babies and hugged Tracy. Getting LaLa and Deuce into their leather spiked harnesses, the two left out of the house to the garage. Bunz handed her future hubby the keys to the matte-black Aston Martin DBX707. The dogs hopped into the rear row of the sleek black and silver accented leather interior. Eric held his woman's hand as she climbed up inside the passenger's side, then went to hop behind the wheel. He started up the twin turbo V8 engines. 707 horses barked out of the sport-tunned exhaust pipes, creating the most luxurious sound that close to a quarter million dollars could buy.

"This muhfucka a beast right here, baby," said Eric, putting it in drive and pulling out of the garage.

"If you like it, then it's yours, E," Bunz told him.

"Oh, I love it, and muchas grassy-ass, 'cause this bitch is dope!"

Bunz laughed as he reached the end if the driveway. Then when Eric banged a left to head to the highway, she asked where they were going.

"Got to holla at the Macho Man. He is in need of our services."

"Back to work already, huh? Well, how 'bout I give you my services to make the trip a little more entertaining," Bunz said suggestively. She reached over to the dash, turned the music up, and blasted A\$AP Ferg and Future's *NEW LEVEL* before she repositioned herself on her knees on the seat.

"Eeeeeee, a nigga finna get blessed again? Okay then!" Eric exclaimed with excitement as his beautiful freak undid his pants, pulled his dick out, and wasted no time lowering her head, mouth open wide, and engulfed him all the way down to his balls. "WOOOO!" he shouted when she started humming, making his balls vibrate.

He reached behind her and cupped her voluptuous ass, squeezing and smacking on it while Bunz deep throated him like sucking dick was what she did best. A minute before Eric reached the junction where 4 Mile Road and Interstate 94 crossed, his eyes rolled to the back of his head, then he groaned gutturally as he busted his nut. Bunz continued sucking until all of his cum was in her mouth. She sat up and swallowed, licking her lips, moaning from the taste of him.

"Maybe I need to disappear again for a few months," he said, coming to a stop at a red light next to where a busy semi-truck wash business was on the side of the road. "I leave and come back to gettin' brain while I'm whippin' an Aston Martin truck 'n shit."

"Eric, if you ever do that shit to me again, my mouth might be the last place you'll want your dick," Bunz told him, narrowing her eyes at him.

The smile fell clean off his face at the meaning behind her words. Bunz busted out laughing at how tripped out he looked.

"You're evil," Eric said, rolling on as the light turned green again.

"You have no idea, but pull some shit like that on me again, E, I swear it on Eric Jr. and Mo-Mo, yo' dick will be in danger, nigga," Bunz told him, then leaned her seat back and kicked back as he hit a left to go up the southbound ramp to 94.

Eric shot south to Illinois. He exited off of 94 at Russell Road, entering truck stop and porn shop city. Down at Frontage Road, Eric hung a left and went past the massive TA Travel Plaza. A minute later, at where the road split to take people to Highway 41 and back to I-94, Eric came up on the big commercial truck and trailer dealership.

Valdez Truck & Trailer Sales was on a banner, fixed to the tall chain link fence that surrounded the property. Entering, Eric and Bunz saw one half of the business had new and used semi-trucks, dump trucks, roll-ff dumpster trucks, and a few other types of heavy duty trucks along with rows of various types of trailers. The other half of the business had rows of custom built trucks and trailers, all of them looking like they could win first place in any truck and car show.

"These niggas really got shit on lock, E," Bunz said to her man as he pulled in and parked next to where a deep blue Bugatti Chiron was parked amongst a sky blue Lamborghini Ventadour SVJ, and a McLaren Senna.

"Smart folks that got rich off moving truckloads of cocaine, literally, make investments that pay off in so many ways that even the Monopoly man would benefit from takin' notes," Eric schooled, as he was schooled by the multi-billionaire drug lords they were paying a visit to.

Bunz adored how in tune with all the pathways to greatness her fiancé was. The ways he had soaked up game instead of ever being one that hated, was the most admirable thing in the world to her. He being such a boss, he was still so humble, and it had shaped her into how she was now.

Eric got out, opened the door for the dogs, then he went around to open the door for his woman. As they headed for the walk-in door at the side of the long pull-in-pull-out service and repair garage, an all-white and chromed out, low-riding Peterbilt rolled past, heading toward the exit. They turned to look, hearing its wickedly powerful engine roaring out of the two monstrous exhaust stacks. The driver behind the wheel, concealed behind darkly tinted windows tooted the custom train horns once, then revved the big caterpillar motor under the hood until flames spat out of the pipes.

"Seein' shit like that makes me wanna traffic yayo all across the country." Bunz chuckled as she and Eric waved at whom they knew to be the queen of Macho Valdez's empire driving the half-million dollar show truck.

***

Eric held the door open for his woman and the dogs. The second they entered the garage, five highly trained canines ran up to them, nothing less than excited to see them. Against the big Rottweiler, the smaller female Rottweiler, the chocolate-reddish tiger striped, Red Nose green-eyed Pit Bull female, the female tiger striped Cane Corso, and the massive male tiger striped Presa Canario, a rare female snow leopard ran up to Eric, Bunz, LaLa, and Deuce.

"I can't believe how big Pablo is," Bunz said as the giant, big-headed dog with dark and light brown bridle fur and clipped ears sniffed at Deuce.

"Well, he's a Mastiff; ain't no such thing as a Mastiff that doesn't get huge. Look at Javi and Michelle's dogs, and Xavier's dog. They all have some killers 'cause of that Bull blood in 'em," Eric explained with detailed knowledge of the rare Bull terrier-blooded Mastiff breeds.

***

Mechanics were working hard on the trucks at the repair and serve stations. Men and women in oily and greasy coveralls created an equal opportunity work environment that every multi-million and multi-billion-dollar company in the Valdez family chain was known to have. The double swinging doors that led to a hallway where the offices were opened up just as Eric and Bunz approached, without their dogs whom had joined the Valdez pack of killers.

"Eeeeeee, look at 'er, joe!" Bunz shouted, super geeked when she saw the Gangsta Boo come through the doors looking like an Instagram model in a sexy black leather Gucci belly-shirt and skirt outfit. She wore spike studded calf-high Christian Louboutin stiletto boots; her long dark hair was flat-ironed and hung loosely down to her shoulders. Her radiant, tattooed, maple-syrup toned skin, highlighted the most distinctively gorgeous, tough-chick look Bunz had ever seen. "Vanessa Rojas in the flesh!" Bunz added, contributing to how everyone said that Gabriela, A.K.A. G-Baby, resembled the feisty former Chicago P.D. cop, played by the actress Lizzeth Chavez.

Eric busted out laughing at the look on the super thick, 5'8" tall Chicago-born Puerto Rican's face as her Cane Corso named Fendi ran up to her.

"You know what, Bunz? If I wasn't so happy to see y'all, I'll kick yo ass," said G-Baby in her sexy, femininely raspy Keisha Cole-like voice.

G-Baby and Bunz hugged, then the Gangsta Boo hugged Eric before leading them to the boss's office.

Chapter 5

Inside the grand luxury car themed office, Bunz and Eric saw the two dread-headed Dominican-Puerto Rican goons of the Steel City Mafia mob, and the inaugurated queen of the Valdez family's massive dynasty. The wild card of the family, Antonio "Macho" Tomás Valdez, was a body builder swole man, standing 6-feet 3-inches tall. His skin was a rich golden-brown, tattooed like Wiz Khalifa. His broad shoulders, barrel chest, and his python-size arms made his very presence an intimidating one. His strong angular jaw, high cheekbones, with his razor sharp beard and baby hair hairline gave him a pretty boy look. His bluish-gray eyes attracted so many women that his wife *and* his girlfriend had to fight with other women to keep them away.

The billionaire god was with his older brother Tool, who stood even taller at 6-feet 6-inches. He had the same golden-brown skin tone, tatted up, muscular like a gym rat, often said to be Dominican-Puerto Rican version of Waka Flocka Flame. Tool was the head honcho of the Steel City Mafia, of which was made up of only seven people, all born and raised in Pittsburgh Steelers territory where the Terrible Towel ruled.

Both of the brawny billionaire cocaine lords were in the office with the remarkably gorgeous Puerto Rican-Colombian gangstress that everyone called ChaCha. She was an Amazon— 6-feet tall beast with body, butter pecan brown skin, long silky hair that was dyed a deep purple. She was amazing, eye-catching, truly alluring. Her soul-piercing Arctic blue eyes were as stunning as Macho's.

ChaCha, older than 35 year-old Macho, his 37 year-old brother, at 39 years old, had been deep in the game of cocaine since he was 18. Although not a blood-born Valdez, she wore the last name proudly with hers. She had married the King of the family after having been the best of friends and lovers on the low. ChaCha had put in so much work that her name rang bells wherever the underworld existed; even in countries she hadn't been to. Having grown up in Pittsburgh, down the street from her husband's family, after her Colombian hitman father and her Puerto Rican dope girl mother relocated with her from Jackson Heights, Queens of New York, ChaCha was as east coast as a hood chick could be. Her money was even longer than Macho's and Tool's.

"My muthfuckin' boy! Easy E!" exclaimed Macho, raising up from behind his titanium, stainless steel and glass desk. "And the queen Bunz! Whaz goodie, yo?"

"Life," Eric replied with a content smile.

"Amen to that, *mano,*" Tool spoke deeply as he and Macho embraced Eric and Bunz.

ChaCha stood up from the long leather couch she had been sitting on, working off of her iPad. She rocked a white t-shirt with New York's Boldest on her chest, tight denim cut-up jeans with 6-inch Louboutin heels on her feet. The super exclusive Bugatti Chiron Blue Sapphire Crystal Tourbillion on her wrist displayed just how up she was. Not many people had watches worth 1.5 million dollars on their wrist, nor the million dollar Richard Mille x McLaren RM40-01 tourbillion on Tool's wrist, and the $800,00 Roger Dupuis x Lamborghini tourbillion on Macho's.

While the men stepped to the side, ChaCha and Bunz embraced like sisters. Since Bunz had met ChaCha, Yessenia, G-Baby, and the other ladies of the Valdez family, Bunz had been treated like family. During Eric's absence, they were there for her and the twins. Once any of them brought someone into the circle, they were family. Those that opposed...they died.

"I can't even begin to express how happy I am for you and the little ones that E's back, mami," ChaCha said, meaning it from the bottom of her heart. "When Macho got taken, and we thought he was dead, yo...it had all of us fucked up in the head, yah'mean, kid?"

Bunz nodded. "It hurt more than I could ever put into words, but he's back; my babies and I have our world back."

"True. Gracias a Dios por eso, ma," ChaCha replied, nodding her head in agreement. "But just so you know, we been havin' a little trouble with some people that buy very large amounts of yayo from us. Antonio and Tool are pissed, as I'm sure Eric's gonna be."

"About what, though?" Bunz asked with a puzzled expression.

"Vente. Macho will explain," ChaCha told her, then they both stepped over to where the guys were tuning in to the fuckery that had been making things very hard for Macho, Tool, ChaCha, her husband, and the others to distribute the Grade A cocaine to their long list of clients around the ILL state.

***

An hour later, Eric and Bunz hopped back into the DBX with LaLa and Deuce. Eric was heated; Bunz was beyond pissed.

"Why it always gotta be some dumbasses that gotta make shit hot for er'body?" Bunz asked as Eric headed towards the exit.

"Muhfuckas is checkin' big stupid bags off the yayo they gettin' from Macho n'nem and still got greedy!" Eric shook his head as he turned out onto the road that led to Route 41. He took a deep breath to calm himself. He was taking it personally, because out of all the craziness plaguing the country, people contributing to the crisis weren't doing anything but causing more death and destruction just to fill their pockets. "Fuck 'em," he said a minute later, merging onto the highway. "Niggas is gon' learn real soon, and I'ma have fun teachin' they asses."

Bunz took his hand into hers. "We are gonna have fun," she corrected, ready to ride with her man.

Eric smiled at her. He kissed her hand, then held it as he cruised the speed limit to head to their next destination.

"Bae?" Bunz then said, feeling upset about the other news they had learned about.

"Yeah?"

Bunz took a deep breath. "Do you think Yvette and Julie are okay?"

Eric inhaled a deep breath of his own, then exhaled. The news of his two dear friends, whom happened to be Illinois State Police officers, along with being known as two bad bitches wit' gunz, being abducted had him sick. He knew that one was pregnant with her first child. While at Macho and Tool's spot, he and Bunz were shown a news clip that painted Yvette as the one that had set her best friend up to get taken. Not a single one of them believed it. Anyone that knew the two state trooper chicks would know that it was them together against the world.

"Until we hear anything more, bae," Eric said, his spirit being attacked by the whole ordeal. "We can't do anything but put up prayers for them. I'll say this though; anybody involved in my two homegirls gettin' taken, if anything happens to them, on my kids…I'm goin' federal on err'body, joe."

"We are goin' federal on everybody, E. Stop leavin' me out of it, nigga."

"Sorry; ya' know what I meant, though. Mufuckas is gon' regret fuckin' around. I swear on all of it."

"Me too, baby," Bunz said, then they both said silent prayers for Yvette and Julie.

***

"You are an evil chick, little cousin," said Marco as he and Leonardo and Tony watched Paula chop and slice body parts with the big meat cleaver.

"Twisted," Leonardo added, looking at what used to be a leg.

"Italian," Tony then said with a chuckle. "You might be just crazy enough to make the cut, Paula."

Paula smirked to herself. "People wanna fuck with me? I'll show everyone," she said, then brought the cleaver down hard on the center of the thigh. "I'm bringin' the days of bloody body parts at the front door in a box back with a F-U note inside, under a big ass smiley face."

WHACK!

She chopped right above the knee. Blood squirted out, splattering onto the lenses of the big scientist goggles she wore with the butcher's apron.

"One of y'all got get me a box," Paula said to her big, brutish cousins. "I have a special delivery to make; Priority Ahipping to Monique Reese Duque and her bitch-ass boyfriend."

Nodding his head to Warren G's *REGULATE* featuring Nate Dogg, Tim pulled up to the rear of Eric and Bunz's beauty salon. He parked behind a neon-green and black Porsche 911 GT3RS and hopped out of his gleaming white Aston Martin DB9 Voltage drop. At the emergency exit door, he entered the code and stepped into the rear supply/stock room and made his way down to the basement.

Beautiful naked ladies, black and Latina, were hard at work. Some were chopping up fresh blocks of crack, others were shaking up pure cocaine, sorting different types of Opioid pill, some were mixing brown sugar and fentanyl with raw heroin. The remaining few had just finished shrink-wrapping bundles of cash that had just been dropped off. It was a sight that always made Tim grin. Thick, sexy women with no clothes on, working hard for their money, even though they all had cake.

Tim walked towards where the head chick in charge stood at a table, working on an Apple MacBook. She was a tatted up chick with skin the same color as honey mustard. The sides of her head were cut low and faded, while the poison green mohawk she rocked her hair in gave her the sexiest edge.

Tazania silently mouthed the words to Lil Wayne's *SHE'S ON FIRE* as it played from her computer through the Bluetooth speaker system in the basement. When she noticed Tim walking towards her, she lit up with excitement. "Heeey," she sang, standing up so that her big breasts were right in his line of sight.

"What's up, baby?" Tim's eyes indeed landed on her succulent melons.

The other women all paused what they were doing and looked at the man they all wanted to fuck, even with him looking like he was fresh out a mental institution.

"Um…what's good? I …um…damn."

Tanzania giggled. She knew how to get a nigga's attention, but so far neither she, nor any of the other women there, had been able to get Tim's attention. "You're here for the re-up for yo' club," Tanzania finished for him.

"Yeah…um…that," he confirmed, still looking at her breasts.

"Well, I can tell yo' ass one thing," she said, stepping around her desk, revealing her full 5'10" coke bottle figure completely bare. "It's not on my chest, Tim."

He froze as she walked up on him, pressing her body against his. Little did Tanzania and the other girls know, Tim wanted to fuck all of them. He was just more focused on getting money than getting pussy. Plus, watching girls practically throw themselves at him was hysterically funny. He heard one of the other ladies catcall, then giggles from a few others. Tim's dick started getting rock hard as the voluptuous belle's candy scented body mist made him want to lick her up and down.

"What's the matter, Timmy?" Tanzania grabbed his crotch, immediately feeling his hardness. "You finally going give up some of that dick all these hoes don't realize belongs to me?"

Tim went to answer, but the second he parted his lips...sounds of gunshots from above started ringing out. Immediately Tim sprang into action. Tanzania quickly grabbed her silk robe and the AK-47 it been hanging over. Her girls followed suit and hurried with their boss and the heart throb to get up to the salon.

Kylie, Cynthia, Amerie, Diedra, Sylvie, and Asia all took cover as the four big men wearing masks shot Thompson Long Guns at the beauty salon. They were glad that they hadn't opened the salon yet, or all the .45 caliber rounds that were flying into the shop would've given all their clients very bad hair days.

"WHO THE FUCK ARE THESE DUDES?" Asia shouted, wishing she could make it to where her Glock 9-millimeter rested in her curling iron drawer.

"I DON'T KNOW!" yelled the shop's manager Kylie. "But THEY ASS FINNA DIE!" She gathered all her courage, hopped up, and ran to the breakroom, coming close to death thirty times in the five seconds it took her to get there. Kylie hurried, grabbed the fully automatic AA12 shotgun with the 20-round drum attached, and ran back out to the shop, ready to show the guys what a bad bitch with a gun could do.

***

Marco, Frankie, Leonardo, and Tony kept blasting their new-age Tommy guns at the shop when gun shots from the outside of the building came flying at them.

"AAGGHH SHIIT!" screamed Frankie when a bullet hit him in the ass.

Marco and the other brothers saw their brother grabbing his ass after his Thompson flew out of his hands. Two more bullets came and slammed into his temple, knocking his brains out the other side. "FRANKIE!" Marco yelled seeing his brother laid out on the ground.

The three turned and saw a big muscular man with two big Desert Eagles popping. Behind him were a mob of women in robes with assault rifles, spitting round after round.

"LET'S GET OUTTA HERE!" Tony yelled, backing up towards the older S-Class Mercedes Benz they'd pulled up in.

BOOM! BOOM! BOOM! BOOM! BOOM! BOOM! BOOM!

Six shotgun blasts rang out. Each one of them hit Tony, blowing chunks of him from his husky frame. He dropped to the ground with gigantic holes spewing out blood. Marco and Leonardo hauled ass towards the Benz as shots came from the salon and the man and mob of girls. They both jumped inside. Marco tried to start the engine but froze when the barrel of the automatic 12-gauge appeared at his window inches away from his head.

"Get out," Kylie demanded with the barrel of her gauge at the man's temple.

Tim went to the passenger's side and smashed the window with one of his .40's. The man in the passenger's seat yelped in pain when glass shards and dust got into his eyes.

CRACK! CRACK! CRACK!

Tim struck him three times in his face with the butt of his cannon. He hit him so hard that the man's face caved in, bones in his face shattering, penetrating his brain.

The man behind the wheel shook, terror stricken. He had spent 31 years on earth with his brothers, and in an instant they were gone. "Kill me! Fuck that shit, ya cunt!" he shouted angrily. "My brothers are dead; my ma and pa are dead! Fuck life! Fuck you!"

Kylie turned her shotgun around and hit him in his jaw with it. In less than a minute, he had the Italian's wrists and ankles bound with jumper cables and tossed him and the other in the trunk. Tanzania jumped in on the passenger's side and started the engine.

"Fuck you doin'?" he asked.

"Fuck it look like? I'm ridin' wit' my nigga! Stop talkin' and let's go!"

Tim slammed it in drive then. Before he hit the gas, Tanzania yelled to her girls to get the merch stashed before the cops arrived, which would be very soon judging by how close the wailing sirens sounded.

***

She watched it all go down from the driver's seat of her Maserati truck parked in the lot of the Metra train station across the street. Furious to see her cousins failed to kill one damn person and destroyed the biggest dope spot her target and her dude had, Paula hit her steering wheel and cursed. She saw swarms of Racine police vehicle speeding into the lot seconds after a few of the girls ran inside, right after the S500 Marco stole peeled off with him and Leonardo in the trunk. Ambulances and a few fire trucks followed entering the bloody crime scene.

Her iPhone ringing took her eyes off the chaos and onto the in-dash LCD screen. Seeing the number to the chick that designed numerous custom pieces of diamond jewelry for her, Paula answered. "This isn't a good time, Karma!" Paula spoke out.

"Oh, my fault. Just lettin' you know I got your new necklace done. Pink and blue sto—"

"BITCH! I SAID IT'S NOT A GOOD TIME! ARE YOU DEAF?" Paula snapped.

"Uh...no."

Paula ended the call. Her eyes began welling up with tears. Anger burned inside of her like an out of control forest fire. She grabbed her phone and made another call, dialing just three numbers.

"9-1-1, what's your emergency?" the dispatcher for the Racine Police Department said when she answered.

"There was a shooting at the little strip store plaza by Highway 20, across from the Metra station," Paula told her.

"We have units already there, ma'am. Are you injured?"

"No, I wasn't there," Paula said, seeing detectives arriving now. "But you should tell your cops at the bottom of the beauty salon they'll find a lot of drugs and cash there."

Paula ended the call without anything else. She looked on towards the scene. She could see one of the detectives pull out their phone and answered the call. Seconds after ended it, Paula saw the detective call a group of uniformed cops and point at the salon. They all ran inside then. Paula smirked to herself.

"There's more than just one way to take a bitch's life," she said to herself ,starting her engine up. "And that consists of taking everything that bitch loves like two little babies."

She put it in drive and pulled off from her perch, ready to get on to her next plan of attack.

Chapter 6

Eric's eyes rolled to the back of his head as Bunz deep throated him while waiting in line in a McDonald's drive thru. Bunz, again, out of nowhere felt the need to please her future husband and never been the type of woman to give a damn about where they got it on at. He palmed her phat ass, caressing it as Bunz took him to the back of her throat over and over again. His toes curled so hard that he thought they would break off in his sneakers.

"Fuck, Monique!" he groaned deeply from his gut.

She moaned her own pleasure from pleasing him. Her pussy was so wet, nipples so hard, aching for some oral stimulation. The whole aspect of when he conducted business turned her on to no end. That boss shit kept her yearning for him every way that a woman whom desired a real man did.

She let his dick out of her mouth and spat on it. She looked up at him and smiled, then went back down, turning up on him. Eric tried so hard to contain himself, but her head game was vicious. He let off of the brake, seeing the car ahead of him move up to the cashier's window. Getting up on the car, he hit the brake a little too hard, screeching to a stop, but Bunz never stopped sucking.

He rolled up to the cashier window when the car in front moved to the pick-up window. The young girl behind the register gasped when she saw Bunz's head bobbing up and down in the man's lap. She saw his face contracting as he groaned. He stuck his arm out the window, waving a $100 dollar bill at her.

"Uh...I can't break that, sir," she said with her lip curled up.

"F-F-Fine! J-Just t-t-t-oooohh shit! T-Take it! Take th-the money!" Eric told her as his nut rose up.

The girl reluctantly took the c-note, slamming her window closed right after. Bunz took his dick out of her mouth and spat on it again. The woman there with their food caught sight of Eric's length before it went back into Bunz's mouth. She gasped, placing a hand over her rapidly beating heart. She looked at Eric when he started groaning loudly.

"Ooohhhhh ssshhhhhiiiit! AAYAAYAAAYAAAA!" he hollered out as he busted his nut.

Bunz used a hand to jerk him while she sucked all of his cum out of him, filling her mouth up with his globby jizz. She lifted her head and spit it all back out onto his cock. The woman watches her slurp it all back up, and moan in bliss as if she was already chomping on the delicious double cheeseburger with strips of bacon on it.

"Oh dear," the lady said, handing Eric the bag. "You two...um...have a wonderful day."

Eric grinned at her as his woman tucked his cock back into his jeans.

"You do the same, ma'am," he replied then rolled away.

The second he got past the window, Bunz busted out laughing at him. Eric shook his head, chuckling though.

"We can never came to this McDonald's again, bae," he told her turning out of the lot and hopping back onto 41 to shoot back north.

"You sayin' you're embarrassed to have gotten yo' dick sucked by the woman you finna marry, in the drive thru of a McDonald's-BP gas station, Eric?" she asked, opening the bag, letting the smell of French fries out.

Eric's phone starts ringing as he passed a truck weigh station. "Not at all, my love," he replied seeing Tim's number on the screen. He answered the call. "Talk to me, young one."

"Fam, it just went down, joe!" His frantic voice filled the Urus up with panic. Even the dogs could sense the hysterics in Tim's voice.

"What happen?" Eric asked.

Tim ran it all down to him. Bunz eyes bugged wide in shock. Eric grew infuriated.

"I'm on the way to the spot right now," Tim told Eric. "Yo, that bitch has to go, fam! Like, straight the fuck up!"

"We on the way," Eric said and ended the call.

No sooner than when he hit *END*, another call came in. he saw the number to the Racine Police Commander pop up. He answered it immediately.

"Yeah?"

"I really hope you have back-up plans for when overzealous detectives possibly find a lot of merchandise, and cash that may not be legal, in a business that is registered in both your name, and your woman's because I am so utterly clueless as to what I can do at the moment."

"Yes, I do. Don't worry, my man," Eric said then he ended the call.

"E…this isn't good, baby," Bunz said worrying about the fact that there had been millions in cash and coke and guns in the salon.

Eric quickly went to make another call.

"We gon' be aight, baby. Trust me," he assured her as ringing came out of the DBX's speakers.

Two rings later, the call was answered, and a smooth baritone voice came out of the speakers.

"What up, lil cutty?" came the voice of the Valdez family boss.

Eric ran everything down to the made man as fast as he could. Bunz stayed quiet, wondering if Danny Valdez actually could do away with something of such federal drug bust level.

"I'm on it yo. Homiez; rest easy," Danny then said before ending the call without another word.

"Is he for real, E?" Bunz asked looking over at him, right as LaLa's nose nudge her left elbow.

"Have you ever known him or anyone else in the fam' to play when it comes to business?"

Bunz chuckled to herself. "Nope; not at all," she answered, then laughed again. "I wonder if he really wants to; if he and his connections could get that racist sex offender out of the presidential race... for good this time."

Eric busted out laughing at his woman. "Real bullets, not high velocity paintballs and shooters that never actually existed?"

"Yup. Take his bitchass to the Everglades 'n let him be gator food," Bunz suggested. "No evidence and no more competition."

"Bae, you gon' be mad at me for sayin' this," Eric then said. "But because all this publicity dude is getting' he gon' win. Watch."

Bunz shook her head. She wanted to debate, but as history showed, when it came down to competition of any kind...the asshole always won.

"You know what? Fuck that clown," Bunz said, and reached over his crotch, undoing his jeans to once again please her man. "His name is banded from our vocabulary. For the next ten minutes, hush it up while I suck on my dick."

Eric chuckled as she got up on her knees in her seat, freeing his stiff cock, lowering her head and taking him all the way to the back of her throat with her ass tooted up high in the air for him to rub and smack on.

"Maan, it feels so g-g-g…oh shit! To be home! WOO!" Eric shouted, reaching around and cupping her plump rear end and caressing it, while she deep throated him.

"Put more, goddammit! Stop skimping on my shit! I want motherfuckers to be so addicted that they all spend every damn dime on my shit!" demanded Booster.

"Bro, this shit already has too much fentanyl in it! Too much of it per ounce will kill our customers instead of bring us more!" Booster's right hand man Ax said as he prepared to mix in more laced heroin with the uncut cocaine they had so much of.

"Fuck that! That's what they want, Ax! To get high that they die! Just do what the fuck I said, or I'll get someone else to do it!" Booster stomped off angrily then, leaving Ax and the two others that were either mixing yayo with the deadly dope or mixing it with crystal meth.

Booster was gung-ho on squeezing every single dime that he could from every gram that he sold. Despite his supplier warning him to stop cutting his product with such poison due to the intense heat it brought upon everyone the Valdez family supplies, but Booster refused. He felt that it was his money that bought his supply, so it was his to do with as he pleased. He wanted the most potent work in Waukegan. He didn't give a fuck about who died because everyone knew that chicks flocked to the dope boys that had that shit that killed.

***

Heading towards his bedroom, Booster heard the sound of glass breaking. Immediately, he pulled his semi-automatic 9-millimeter Smith & Weston and took the safety off. He crept towards the bedroom where he heard the glass break. Coming to the first bedroom, Booster slowly peaked around the corner of the doorway. He peeped into the bare room and saw a brick on the carpeted floor with broken shards of glass around it.

"Man, what the fuck?" he said to himself, walking towards the smashed out window.

The second he got within five feet of the window, Booster's eyes bugged wide as he saw a huge dog flying right at him.

"OOHH FUUCK!" he screamed in panic as the dog took him to the floor and starts mauling him.

The next thing Booster knew, another dog jumped inside and started attacking him. He cried for help as two sets of teeth; powerful jaws clamped down on both of his calf muscles.

"HEEEELP! AAXX! ROOOB! JAAAY! SOMEBODY!" he cried.

Then one of the dogs ripped his calf muscle clean off from his leg, causing him to scream out at the tops of his lungs.

"Y'all hear yo' boss? It sounds like he's in a lot of pain," Eric said, as Bunz kept the Draco up, ready to blow Ax, Rob and Jay down.

"W-W-We tried to tell him, man! I know who the shit c-came from!" Ax stammered, feeling his guts bubbling so much that he was about to shit his pants. "Booster's a greedy dude, man!"

Just as Ax had finished his sentence, Deuce came into the kitchen, with Booster's hand in his mouth. LaLa was still chewing on the man's fleshy calf muscle when she entered behind her mate.

"Well damn!" Eric laughed at his dogs. "They been doin' this shit for so long, a nigga ain't e'en gotta tell 'em what to do!"

"Good job, LaLa and Deuce!" praised Bunz.

They both started wagging their tails. Deuce dropped Booster's hand on the linoleum tile floor. With his gloved hand, Eric picked it up, then went to Ax.

SMACK!

He swung the hand and smacked Ax in his face, then went and smacked Rob, then Jay with it. Bunz laughed at them.

"Check it out; yo' boss is gonna die. Bae," Eric said, giving her the go ahead.

She walked off without another word. Deuce followed her, while LaLa stayed with Eric.

"As for y'all, I'ma leave it up to my fiancée when she—"

"NO WAIIT!"

BRRRRRR! BRRRRRR! BRRRRRR!

Eric smiled at the sound of his girl haunching the business like a G. "Come back," he then finished.

"Please, man!" Rob begged, tears falling, snotty nosed, pants wet. "We ain't have no say-so in it! Booster ran the show!"

"Not anymore he doesn't," said Bunz as she came back with Deuce.

"I told these followers that I was leavin' it up to you to decide if they walk up outta here today," Eric told her, still holding Booster's hand.

"Come on! Please, miss! We won't do none of that shit again!" Jay swore.

"I truly believe you won't because you won't be able to," Bunz said. She didn't even hesitate to dump the three. She wet them all up, painting the wall behind them crimson.

"FUCK TRUMP!" Bunz then shouted at the slumped dope boys.

Eric laughed so hard that he started coughing and choking like he had just took a puff of the most potent exotic weed on earth. "Holy shit! Bae, yo' ass is certified crazy, joe! On God!" Eric said.

Bunz shrugged. "You made me mad by sayin' Trump gon' win, so I was just releasin' my frustrations."

"I got somethin' you can release some more of them frustrations on when we get back to the crib," Eric told her with a mischievous grin on his face.

Bunz started smiling back at him. "Sounds like we should finish up here and get goin'. Don't you think?"

"Indeed, I do," Eric agreed.

They both ransacked the house then. Within a half hour, they had found a hidden trap spot in the floor of the bathroom. Stacks of cash were stashed in it; Eric took it all.

Bunz found a couple of bars of gold, both weighing ten pounds each. Right after, she discovered nine kilos of cocaine that seemed to glow from how white the powder was from inside the plastic wrap. Eric came with a brown paper shopping bag that had the half brick that Booster's guys were fluffing up, wrapped in a black garbage bag.

"What sayeth of thine bricks of pow-pow?" Bunz asked Eric.

"By word of thy Steel City Mafia brethren, taketh thee and distribute thee to thee of no payment in thy flesh," Eric told her.

Bunz busted out laughing.

"And our dear law enforcement sisters would likely live to have this," he added, holding up the bag with the deadly cutters in it.

"Yvette and JuJu been pretty busy lately," Bunz said, pulling out all the bricks and tossing them onto the nearby bed. "They got tied up in some shit with one of their own cops."

"I heard. Be prepared to have our problem-solving services requested by them," Eric said, knowing at some point the two wild Illinois state trooper chicks were going to war, and could definitely use the help of every soldier in their circle.

Chapter 7

"BA-DA-DA-DA-DAAA!" sang out Tim, then *SMACK!*
Naked, hands tied behind his back, ankles bound to the legs of the metal chair, Marco cried from the sting caused by getting hit again by the partially frozen fish.
CRACK! CRACK! BINK! WHAM!
Tanzania socked Marco up, hitting him with a left, a right, a jab, then a hard uppercut. Three of his teeth flew out of his mouth.
"You ready to talk yet?" Tim asked him.
Marco glared up at him, sneering. "Vaffanculo!"
"I do not know what that means," Tim said.
SMACK!
He fished Marco's face again.
CRACK!
Tanzania jawed him again.

"HO INTENZIONE DI UCCUDERTI!" Marco shouted angrily.

"You just called me dirty?" Tim asked.

SMACK! SMACK! SMACK!

Tim smacked him three more times. The fish broke in half. "Aw, man, this punkass bitch broke my fish!" Tim groaned. "Now I'm really mad."

"Allow me, baby," Tanzania said. She socked Marco up repeatedly, unleashing all of her anger, but no matter how many times she punched him, the man refused to give his sister up. "This muthafucka right here, man," Tanzania said, shaking her head at the man's resilience. "Where's LaLa and Deuce when they're needed?"

Tim shook his own head, agreeing with Tanzania. "I'm gettin' real tired of you, bruh. You 'bout to make me gut cho' bitchass like a fuckin' pig," Tim swore to him.

"And cook yo' fat ass! Bitch!" snapped Tanzania.

CRACK!

Tim delivered a devastating right hook to his jaw.

"Talk, fatty, or I'ma give yo' ass GD glasses!" Tanzania promised.

"Fuck you, whore!" Marco spat, then spat a wad of phlegm at her feet.

"Oh no the fuck you did not just do that nasty ass shit!" she gasped, disgusted by the sight if it on the ground.

Tim went over to where the old wooden table with a multitude of tools was. He grabbed a machete, glanced back over at Tanzania with a smirk. "Bet you that this will make him talk," he told her right as she was about to grab a pair of sheers and cut Marco's nipples off.

Tanzania fell back at Tim's words. She watched him go to where Marco's dead brother laid on a steel table. With the razor sharp cutter in his hand, Tim went to Leonardo's side. Tanzania and Marco both watched as Tim took the dead man's arm and sliced it off. Marco's swelled up eyes filled with tears seeing his brother being hacked apart. He continued looking. He watched the guy slice the hand off at the wrist, then he chopped each finger off. Collecting them, he watched the man turn back to him with a demented smirk.

Tanzania stood motionless by the man, wondering what in God's name Tim was planning to do with the several fingers. Tim walked up to Marco and punched him in his stomach. Marco yelped out in pain. Tim slammed one of Leonardo's fingers into his mouth and forced his mouth shut. Marco's eyes bugged wide as he tasted the bloody finger of his brother in his mouth.

"SWALLOW IT BITCH!" Tim shouted and smacked him in his throat, forcing Marco's esophagus into action.

Marco swallowed his brother's pointer finger. Tim kept on, hitting him hard in places that made him scream out in pain, forcing a finger in his mouth, then smacking his throat.

"Wow...this nigga is fucking crazy," Tanzania said to herself, catching chills up her spine.

"Tell me what I wanna know or I'ma cut his heart out and make you eat that like you're Montezuma," Tim told Marco.

Just then, the door to the room opened. In walked Eric, Bunz, and their XXL Bullies. Eric and Bunz saw the battered Italian in the chair and the other one, minus an arm, laid out in the table.

"Proceed," Eric told Tim.

He and Bunz and the dogs hung back and let Tim work.

"You got somethin' to say yet?" he asked Marco.

"Y-Y-Yeah!" the man shouted, feeling sick to his stomach at the fact that he had just been force-fed his own brother's fingers.

"Well, let's hear it, bitch. Where is your sister?" Tim asked.

Marco looked at him. "At y-your...momma's house, b-bitch!"

Eric shook his head. While Tim started punching Marco up, he went to the wall of tools. He grabbed a small ice cream scooper, went to the dead man, and scooped one of his eyes out.

"Step aside, young grasshopper," he told Tim, making his way over to help.

Tim stepped back. The ladies and the dogs watched as Eric took the eye out of the scooper and held it so the still alive Italian could see it.

"You see this eye, my man?" he asked, looking at Marco. "It sees you. Ever taste a human eyeball?"

Marco looks into Eric's eyes and suddenly grew terrified. There was something demonic about the braided up thug that had him close to shitting his pants.

"Tell me where your sister is and not only will you not have to eat your brother's eye, but you will not be hurt."

"Sh-Sh-She lives in L-Lake Forest!" Marco told.

Eric turned and grinned at Tim. "See how that works?" he asked, then turned back and stuffed Leonardo's eyeball in Marco's mouth making him chew it up and swallow it.

Tanzania cringed, almost puking up the Jimmy Dean sausage-egg-n-cheese sandwich she had for breakfast. Bunz smirked, mentally cheering her fiancé on.

Tim shook his head. "Why didn't I just do that instead of the fingers?" he asked more to himself.

"Fingers are okay, youngster," Eric said, pulling out his snub-nosed .357 revolver. "But what's more nastier than forcing someone to chew up a raw human eyeball?" He thumbed the hammer back and pointed it at Marco's face.

"Y-You said you wasn't gon' hurt me, man!" he cried.

"I know," Eric replied.

POW!

One slug, close range, obliterated Marco's head.

"Did that hurt?" Eric leaned close to the headless corpse, listening closely. "Oh. No answer. Guess I did keep my word." He rose back up, dug in Marco's pocket finding his phone in it. He went to the contacts and found Paula's number. He called it, putting it onto speaker mode.

"Marco! What the hell happened!" Paula snapped as she answered.

"Well. First and foremost, Marco's dead, and so are the other three," Eric said.

Bunz, Tim, and Tanzania stayed quiet. Silence came from the phone.

"I imagine that your silence means you were not expectin' this. So, to further avoid me havin' to kill more of your family, how about you bring yo' thot ass to me. I'll even let my woman handle you. If you fight her heads up and win, we fall back. If you lose, then I will stuff you in an oven and cook yo' dumbass."

There was more silence for half a minute. They all waited to hear a comeback. Seconds later, they heard Paula start to laugh. Her laughter became hysterical. Eric and the others all furrowed their eyebrows looking at each other.

"That bitch is really nuts," Bunz said to herself.

"You really are stupid, Mr. Problem Solver, aren't you?"

"How do you mean, Miss Dick Smoker?" Eric replied.

"I was raised in the mob, dude. Shit happens. Plans don't always go as expected, which is why you should always have a backup plan."

"I agree," Eric said.

"Somebody wants to say hello to you," Paula then said.

Eric listened as the sound of ruffling came out of the phone.

SMACK!

"Say hi, bitch," they all heard Paula say.

Eric and Bunz then heard Tracy's voice.

"E-Eric…I-I'm sorry!" she cried.

Paula's voice came back as Eric and Bunz both nearly felt their hearts drop out of their asses.

"You two have the cutest babies. Twins, right?" she asked.

They could hear Eric Jr. and Monique start to cry just then. Tim and Tanzania were both speechless, shell-shocked as they realized that somehow Tracy and the twins had been taken and were now in Paula's possession.

"I imagine that your silence says that you were not expecting this," Paula said, throwing Eric's words back at him. "So, this is how it's gonna go, bitch! I am going to keep taking people you love, and I am going to send them to you in pieces. And there is no bargaining, no negotiating. Everyone you care about is going to die. Even those fat ass dogs you have. Buh-bye now, bitch!"

The call went dead. Eric stood there, frozen. Bunz's eyes filled with tears. She shook her head, unable to believe that the bitch really had her babies and Tracy.

Tim and Tanzania were filled with dread. Neither of them felt like they could even breathe.

"Not my babies! Please, God, not my babies!" Bunz cried as she slowly began to lose it.

Eric ran to her, catching her before her knees gave out. She burst into tears in his arms, wailing loudly as the seriousness of the situation hit her like a speeding Mack truck.

"What are we gonna do, E?" Bunz pleaded to know. "She has our babies and Tracy!"

"I know, baby, I know," Eric told her, holding her tightly in his arms. "We'll figure it out. This will not be the end of any of them," he declared, but even he was unsure of how to go about finding them; let alone getting them back.

***

Paula smirked as she ended the call. She looked at Tracy who was holding the crying babies. Sitting in the back of the old box truck, she was more afraid for the infants than her own life. She couldn't believe that she had gotten caught off-guard so easily. A simple trip to the store for some groceries turned into a kidnapping. A group of men in black looking like secret service had surrounded her car. She tried to hurry up and get the kids up out of there, but only to discover that her battery had been disabled. Her window was smashed. She was yanked out, cut up by broken glass. The babies were taken out of their baby seats, and they were carted off to the beach up in Kenosha, Wisconsin. Tracy could not understand how Paula had found her, and it had her even more afraid not knowing what the little Italian chick was capable of.

***

"What now, boss?" asked Dominic, her new head of security and ex-Navy Seal that had been hired from his top-notch reputation, and his fearless team of mercenaries.

"Take them from her," Paula told him.

"Wait, wait, wait! No!" Tracy shouted, clutching Eric Jr. and Monique tightly in her arms, stepping to the rear wall of the box truck's cargo hold, where a little window looked out into the cab.

Two of Dominic's guys climbed up into the cargo section to take the wailing twins. Tracy tried to put up a fight, but a rock-hard Flintstone fist to her jaw sent her to the floor seeing stars.

The men took the babies from her and hopped out. Another stepped up with two grenades in his hands. Still laid out, Tracy saw the two explosives in his hands.

"It's been real, girl," Paula said to Tracy as the man pulled the pins out and tosses them inside. "Say hi to Aundrea when you get there!" she added.

The door was yanked down. Paula and her men took off running. Seven seconds later…

BOOM!

The grenades exploded. The box truck shot up into the air, a big ball of fire, and landed on its side.

"Alrighty, then, Mr. Dominic," Paula said as they headed towards where Paula's executive-edition built Range Rover Supercharged sat parked by Dominic's early 2000 Ford

Excursion. "We have a flight to catch. Let's get these little ones used to real Italians."

Dominic nodded his head. "Copy that, boss," he replied walking behind her, eyeing her perky little ass, loving how her cheeks wiggled in the tight read leather dress she was wearing.

Paula was assisted up into the SUV's boss styled rear by Dominic, then secured inside. Once the driver pulled off, she leaned back and smiled. "It feels soooo good being such a sexy and untouchable queen," she told herself, feeling triumphant, while dying for her targets to discover the next surprise she had for them.

***

Eric, Bunz, Tim, and Tanzania, all stood a hundred feet away from the front porch of Bunz's house. LaLa and Deuce stayed at their side but were growling at the sight that had them all stuck and staring. A long cardboard box sat on the porch. The bottom of it was red and wet, leaking like raw meat being left sitting on a hot side walk. Tears filled Bunz's eyes. Eric held her in his arms. Tanzania stayed silent. She didn't know what was in the box, but judging how the others looks as if they were about to discover Jesus Christ inside the box; she knew they felt someone of great importance was inside.

Tim went up to the box. He took a deep breath and prayed that it was just a dead deer or cat inside and not her, the woman he had fell so deep in love with, that it had been hard to breathe without her around. Eric, Bunz, and Tanzania watched silently as Tim lifted the top of the box off. He looked inside and froze. For about ten seconds, he just stared. Bunz went to the steps, fearing the worst. When she got to where Tim stood stuck, she saw why. Inside the box was a body with no head, but the arms and legs were cut off and stuffed inside. For just a fraction of a second, Bunz felt relief that since there was no head, that it was possible that it wasn't Andrea. Her hope disappeared when she noticed the same thing Tim had: the heart shaped tattoo that Andrea had above the middle of her breasts.

"FUUUUUUUUUUCK!" Tim yelled as his tear-filled eyes turned demon red.

Bunz burst into tears, crying her eyes out, sinking down to her knees. Eric ran over and saw the mutilated body inside the box. Tim broke down sobbing loudly as did Bunz. Eric's own eyes filled with tears as grief overwhelmed him.

Still standing by LaLa and Deuce, Tanzania shed tears from seeing the anguish her people were feeling. Not knowing what to say, Eric sank down and put his arms around Tim and his woman. All he could think to do was try and comfort them. He hadn't had the chance to meet Andrea, but having been told a lot about the young soldier, Eric's heart broke for her. For the first time in a long time, he cried.

Chapter 8

Month Later...

The undercover detective nodded his head, listening intently as Nick revealed all. Sitting in the dark gray Dodge Charger, Detective Rodriguez recorded Nick Borjes as he informed on a big family of cocaine traffickers and dealers along with paid killers.

"So, I've heard a lot about this family," Detective Rodriguez told Nick as he watched a few cars go past to park in a section close to a playground. "My question to you is why risk your life to do this? If you know them as well as you say you do, then you should know they've likely got law enforcement in their pockets, Nick. There are cops out there that would cross the line in the blink of an eye for $100K in cash, just to pop a snitch."

Nick looked at the old Puerto Rican man that he'd been confidential informant for, for nearly five years. "What'chu sayin', Rodriguez?" asked Nick with a hand resting on his waist where the butt of his Glock was covered by his Versace shirt, his eyes shifting around as he was expecting a set up to happen.

"Relax, Nick. If I was one of whom I spoke of, don't you think I'd have patted you down and took that gun you think I didn't notice you have?"

Nick turned and looked back at the old cop. He sighed, taking a deep breath to calm his nerves. He knew what he was doing was very bad and eventually would come to the light. "Look, Rodriguez. I got a target on my back now, and I need to get out of town! Do you have my money or what?"

"Yes. It's on the trunk," the detective told him. Rodriguez reached down to pull the trunk lever. "I will advise you against trying to fuck a billionaire drug lord's baby sister in the future, Nick," he said as Nick got out of the car. "And stop snitching!"

Mamate un bicho, puto! Nick thought to himself as the detective's last words flew out of the unmarked car before he closed the door.

Glancing around the park, Nick saw the young children playing at the playground. At the baseball diamond, and intense game between the teams of local park district residents had cheers filling the air. Nick looked all around and saw nothing that seemed out of place. He went to the trunk, open it, and saw the bag there. Unzipping it, he saw stacks of cash inside. Nick grabbed the bag, closed the trunk, and rushed off to where his tinted white 2000 Ford Mustang SVT Cobra R sat, looking like a four-wheel jet with an angry front end. He jumped inside the wickedly fast 2-door as the Charger pulled off. With his keys out, Nick closed the door and inserted the key into the ignition. The supercharged V8 crank over, growling out of the high performance exhaust pipe that jetted out of the sides of the car. Nick shifted the 6-speed into 1st and pulled off, dipping out of the park with haste. He had $150,000 in the bag to add with the money he'd saved up working one of the drug warehoused, owned by the Valdez family.

Coming to a red light at Sheridan Road and Yorkhouse Road, Nick paused behind a dump truck. Nodding his head to Rick Ross, Nick's eyes continued shifting around, his nerves jumped up. He couldn't wait to get to his house, grab the rest of his loot, and get gone. His plans to go back to Ponce had him anxious and excited. Living in Puerto Rico, a kid had been great. Going back there a rich man, he was already seeing sexy ladies vying for him, everywhere he went.

Smiling at the visual of phat juicy Boricua booty cheeks clapping on his face, Nick suddenly felt a hard bump from behind. "The fuck," he snapped when he saw a big semi-truck behind him had rear-ended his prized Mustang. "Hijue puta! Drunk-ass truck driver!"

He went to get out and go knock some sense into the trucker when the big rig started pushing his car forward.

"AYE! AAAYYYE! WHAT THE FUUUCK!" he shouted as the front of his car reached the rear of the dump truck.

The rig pushed Nick's car, crumpling it as if it was a beer can. Nick tried to open the door, but the car's frame bending in stopped him from being able to open it. The windows and windshield shattered. Nick screamed in panic. The Mustang started bending upwards in the middle, his knees got pinned at the dashboard, bent inwards. Nick cried as something shocked. Dug into his right kneecap, drawing blood. He closed his eyes, praying for it to stop. Then the semi stopped pushing. He opened his eyes, hands wrapped tightly around the steering wheel. He looked around frantically. His knees were still pinned. He couldn't move. The pain from whatever was stabbing his kneecap was unbearable.

Click-Clack.

The side that he was all too familiar with came. He looked to his left and saw a man with long braids wearing a ski mask was pointing a long pistol with a pyramid shaped barrel at him.

BOOM!

Eric pulled the trigger. The massive .50 caliber Desert Eagle Semi auto spat blue flames as the bullet flew out of the barrel and exploded the target's head. His brain spread all over the inside of the crumpled car. Blood dripped from the ceiling. The headless corpse tremble as the nerves in each limb jumped. Seconds later, the body went limp. Eric lowered his gun then looked at the creepy old Peterbilt behind the Mustang. Behind the wheel, Macho nodded his head.

In the old Kenworth that had the dump trailer in front of the Mustang, Eric looked to his left as Tool opened the door, poking his head out. Eric gave him a thumbs up, then hurried across the street and jumped into his torture van, ready to get to the next target.

"Relax, goddammit! Those people are freaking multibillionaires! What person do you know that is stupid rich like they are will miss a few hundred grand?" Wallace shot back when his wife Sheena grew frantic about him syphoning money from one of the business accounts he managed. "Especially when the one whom would know is me!"

Sheena's heart raced in her chest. She was petrified to the point that she literally felt sick. At any moment, she felt like her bowels would evacuate, and the entire restaurant that she and her husband were dining in would clear out from her. She could barely eat. Her appetite was gone, vanished after noticing $635,000 added to their private joint account. Even with how many business accounts her accountant husband managed; she knew he wasn't bringing in wop loads of money like that. She asked him about it when they were seated inside the new Caribbean cuisine eatery. She pleaded with him to explain how they had amassed more than $5 million in the last three months when he only made $100,000 to $175,000 a year.

What really had Sheena close to shitting on herself was the fact that her husband managed hundreds of millions of dollars that belonged to a lot of people that were a part of certain underworld organizations. The type of underworld organizations that were lawless and would shed the blood of entire families to get their point across.

"Wallace! The rich stay rich because they know how to watch their money! They do have people that watch the people that watch and manage their money!"

"Enough, Sheena!" Wallace demanded sternly, immediately silencing his wife. "I don't want to hear anything else about it, dammit! I know what I'm doing! Period!"

Sheena refrained from arguing any further. It was pointless. She married a man that was too macho to listen to a woman's warning. She picked her fork back up and stabbed a slice of her Santorini lamb, stuffing it into her mouth. *I'm divorcing this idiot. I am not going to get myself killed because he wants to be greedy. Fuck him,* Sheena thought to herself.

A waitress came up to the table just then. On a silver tray, she had a bottle of Dom and two crystal flutes.

"Oh, we didn't order this," Wallace told her when she sat it on the table.

"This comes from the lady and the gentleman over there," the beautiful brown Latina told him, setting a flute in front of Wallace and in front of Sheena.

The husband and wife duo looked at where the waitress was pointing. Through the crowded restaurant, they saw a man with a neat bald-fade haircut and beard sitting with a gorgeous chick with a green mohawk. The guy smiled and held up a flute of his own. The girl did as well.

"Do you know them?" Sheena asked her husband.

"Uh…not sure."

"Says you manage one of his business accounts," the waitress told him, "and wants to thank you for the great job you've done."

Wallace turned and gave the guy a smile and a nod. "See?" he said to his wife as the waitress poured them both full flutes of bubbly. "The people I manage love my work. You're worrying yourself about nothing, dear."

Sheena sighed, indeed feeling a little bit of relief. She managed to smile and nod her head.

"I need to use the restroom. I'll be right back," Wallace said, standing up and walking off.

Sheena took a sip of her champagne and watched her husband until he turned the corner and disappeared from her line of sight.

Wallace drained his bladder then went to wash his hands. As he lathered them up with foam soap, the bathroom door opened up. In walked the man that had been sitting with the green haired chick. "Oh. Hey, thanks for the—"

Wallace's words stopped abruptly when the man whipped out a semi-automatic 9-millimeter fitted with a silencer. "I have a message from Yessinia Moralez-Valdez," the man said with fire in his blue eyes, finger wrapped around the trigger.

PFFT! PFFT! PFFT! PFFT! PFFT! PFFT! PFFT!

Wallace jerked as slugs hit him up. Each shot put him up against the wall. The final bullet sailed through his forehead, exiting out the back of his head. He slid down to the floor. A trail of blood on the wall was left behind.

The shooter smirked, looking at his handiwork. "You're fired...bitch ass nigga," Tim said to the corpse. He tucked his gun back into his waistline and fixed the bottom of his shirt over it. Without a word more, he left out the bathroom to get back to Tanzania and get on to the next one.

"Your husband is not coming back. Leave and move on with your life before you lose it."

Sheena looked up at the green haired woman. Her facial expression told a story that was a mile long.

"Am...Am I s-safe?" she asked, stammering over her words.

"Yes. You are," she said just as the man she'd been sitting with returned, walking up behind her and wrapping his arms around her waist.

"Ready, love?" Sheena heard the man ask the voluptuous woman.

"For the world, babe," Green Hair replied, then to Sheena, "Peace to you, Sheena Robertson."

The two took their leave then. Sheena watched them from her window hop into a box-shaped Chevy Caprice with big chrome rims on it. Just as the blue-eyed man pulled off, shouts of panic about a dead man in the bathroom came instantly, causing pandemonium to break out.

"Wow...you are amazingly beautiful! Good God!" said Travis Nolan of Nolan Transport, LLC, completely stunned by the impeccably dressed woman.

At first, he was highly upset when his secretary buzzed him, telling him a representative from an opposing trucking firm was there to speak with him. It was the third one that week. The $185-million-dollar oil field contract he had used political connections to get, rather than go about obtaining it the right way, had a lot of people upset. Travis didn't give a rat's ass though. He had friends in high places that proved to be very useful whenever he needed them.

When he sat back in his butter-soft leather high back chair behind his custom glass and gold-framed desk in the comforts of his big corner office with floor-to-ceiling windows looking out over downtown Dallas, Travis had been expecting another cowboy hat, suit and cowboy boot-wearing redneck to come through the door. Instead, a woman with creamy white skin, Asian facial features and with long silky blonde hair that was flat-ironed bone-straight entered. She seemed taller than the average female in the sexy white pointed toe Christian Louboutin stiletto pumps she wore. Her voluptuous body was shocking to Travis, who had not seen an Asian woman so tall and fine. Add to that, the brown long-sleeved top she wore fit so tightly that her breasts looked like melons. With it, she wore a very short, very tight chocolate brown and beige plaid mid-thigh length skirt. Her legs glistened from a fresh wax and lotion. Her makeup was minimal, but still her natural beauty was enhanced by it and the gleaming diamond jewelry she had on.

She entered his office carrying an alligator skin briefcase. The smile on her face was both cheerful and determined. Travis could tell she was on a mission. As he drank the beautiful woman in, a mission of his own developed in his head.

"Why, thank you, Mr. Nolan," she said, closing his door behind her, locking it. "Flattery will get you everywhere, if you do it right."

Travis heard the seduction in her voice as she spoke. The girl nearly purred, oozing sexuality. "I, uh, I've never had a complaint, my dear," Travis replied, playing right along with her flirtatious mannerisms.

She smiled. Walking towards the two chairs in front of his desk, she introduced herself. "My name is Mai Ling Chang, Mr. Nolan, and I've been sent here by my boss to speak with you about the—"

"Oil field contract that people think I stole," he finished for her.

She giggled, setting her briefcase on his desk and opening it up. "I am here about that, but my boss isn't concerned with how you got it. He respects when a man goes after what he wants, Mr. Nolan." She lifted the top, then looked at him over the ledge. "That is the type of man you are, right? The type that goes after what he wants?"

"Yes, Miss Chang, I am. Especially when it comes to a lovely woman that radiated beauty."

"Is that so, Mr. Nolan?" She walked around his desk and sat on the edge, positioning herself so provocatively that when she overlapped her right leg over her left, he could see up her skirt…and she was not wearing panties.

His eyes were glued to her womanhood. His mouth watered. She smelled like chocolate, and he found himself wondering what she tasted like. "Yes." Travis brazenly placed a hand on her thigh, caressing her soft skin. "You know, I may be willing to split the contract with your boss, if you convince me that'll it'll be...worth my time," he told her, licking his lips.

The woman unlapped her leg, then she tossed her left up and over his head so that both of her legs were wide open in front of him. Travis' eyes went wide. He licked his lips at the sight of pussy up her skirt just inches away from his face. Ready to go in and get it, he went to move forward to get a whiff of her goodness gracious when suddenly her legs closed around his neck and started squeezing.

Travis, thinking it was some sort of foreplay, chuckled at first, until she went python on him. "Hey? Wh-What are you doing!"

Through a clenched teeth smile she said, "I am showin' you the type of chick that goes after what she wants, and what I want is the $2-million put over yo' head by my bro Macho Valdez. But," she said squeezing even harder, making him struggle to breathe while trying to pry her strong legs loose... "in order for me to get that money, you, my good man... you have to die!"

Travis heard the name and instantly caught the runs. He tried again to pry her vice gripped legs from around his neck. He could barely breathe; his brain was losing oxygen fast. He felt light headed. In a last effort to save himself, Travis attempted to lift up and slam the girl down on the desk hard enough to rattle her and make her let go. She had anticipated it and pulled a move of her own before he could. With all of her might, she twisted her body to the left with such quickness and power that it snapped Travis neck instantly. The light in his eyes faded. His body went limp. She let go of him. His body dropped to the floor.

Bunz got off of the desk and kicked his head, making sure his neck was broke. When he didn't move, she was sure he was dead. Quickly then, she got to part two of the job. She went to her briefcase and grabbed the little computer flash drive she had brought. Hurrying to where his computer was, Bunz plugged the data-storage device into the USB port, then she started rummaging around, searching the files on the hard drive.

"Yes! Bingo!" she said to herself when she located the file she needed, of which Travis had attempted to disguise as *Family Memorabilia.*

Opening it, Bunz saw all of the contracts that Travis had snaked from other big companies, which even included Valdez Industries, Inc., the multi-billion dollar empire built by Macho's two greatest uncles and grandfather back in the 70's. Bunz quicky uploaded the file onto her flash drive.

Storing it back into her briefcase, Bunz clicked off the communications signal jammer that she had been given to keep anyone from calling for help, closed the briefcase, then made her way out. She walked right past all the people in the office that were too busy on their computers to notice her, even with her high heels clacking loudly on the floor. Bunz made it back to her stolen rental car and hopped in. The second she pulled off, she got a call from Eric.

"Meet me in the A, baby. We got somethin' else to handle, and I mean ASAP," he told her.

"I'm on the way," Bunz told him then ended the call.

She sent a text to Macho about the mission, concluding it with *Problem solved, big bro!* and a smiley face emoji. She made a stop at a post office, mailed the flash drive to the P.O. box Yessy told her about, then Bunz parked the steamer where her own legit rental car was and headed to the airport.

Chapter 9

Hours Later...

Sitting outside of the Botanical Garden in Atlanta, Bunz sat quietly next to Eric in a black Chevy Malibu with dark tints. They both waited for their target to appear. After Eric explained the job, Bunz learned that it was not a random person, but one that had been connected to people very dear to Eric that had become dear to her as well.

Tears had filled her eyes when Eric told her what he had recently learned about Yvette and Julie. It had her so angry that she was close to crying.

"Do you think this is gonna work, bae?" Bunz asked as her voice broke up.

Eric sighed. "I hope; I still can't even believe this bitch ass nigga got down on his own woman like that, much less her home girl and a cat that's supposed to be his mans."

"That's some snake ass shit," Bunz said, shaking her head.

Minutes later, Eric peeped the black Mercedes S580 Maybach Benz the target had been reported to be whipping since his arrival in ATL. Eric put his leather gloves on and grabbed the two custom made pistols that resembled Glocks made of a material that would not set off metal detectors. Bunz grabbed her ceramic knife and tucked it into her tight cut up jeans. They got out of the car and headed towards the entrance once they saw the man and the woman he was with that was pushing a baby stroller.

***

Denise could feel her heart pounding in her chest as the rich gangster sitting across from her spit words full of passion and sincerity. She wanted nothing more at the moment but to jump on him and kiss him. She couldn't recall a man ever looking at her the way T.G. was. The look in his eyes was that of a man that was falling…hard.

"You are a king, T.G. For the fact that you can admit wrong doings, and how I can actually see remorse in your eyes. I know you are for Letoya and me."

T.G. couldn't hide his smile. She had just spoke some real shit, and it made him feel like he wasn't completely a piece of shit. "You hungry?" he asked her then.

Denise nodded her head yes.

"Aight. Lemme go hit the head and we'll shoot to this lil spot I Googled," T. G. told her.

He got up and left, catching sight of the very beautiful woman with rich gold dreadlocks, smooth brown skin, rocking a black shirt that had a duffel bag overflowing with cash across her chest, tight jeans with cuts that showed off her thick thighs, wide hips, and without a doubt a phat round ass. The spike-toed pumps on her feet clacked loudly on the floor as she walked past him. She cast a glance at him as they passed each other that made T.G. unable to help take a second look. Glimpsing such a phatty he almost ran into a man in a Balmain fit, rocking big diamond jewelry and cornrows in his head. T.G. begged the guy's pardon and made his way to the bathroom.

Eric waited, standing against the door to the men's room. By the time the target had realized he was in there, it was way too late for him to save himself. With his cannons out, Eric watched him flush the toilet. When he turned around and saw Eric there his eyes went wide, jaw dropped, looking like his heart had just dropped out of his ass.

"What up, homeboy? You and I are gonna have a chat," Eric told him. "If you lie, you will die. Period. Got it?"

T. G. nodded his head.

"Good. Wash yo' hands first. I can't talk to a nigga that just took a leak and hasn't washed his hands."

T.G. washes his hands, then faced who he assumed was going to be turning his lights out.

"Where is Yvette and JuJu?" Eric asked, looking right into T.G.'s eyes, knowing that eyes never lied.

"I swear; I don't know fam. The cop that kept tryna get at her, he…" T.G. took a deep breath, finding it beyond difficult to speak the truth. But it was either come clean or get slumped. "He and his bitch came at me wit' enough dirt to probably get me the death sentence."

Eric nodded his head but was far from understanding how a man could deliver his own woman into the hands of an incredibly dirty cop that had the sickest obsession with her. "You a bitch, fam," Eric told the man. "I do not just say that because I got guns. Any nigga that gets down on women is a trick ass, bitch ass nigga. On God."

The guy said nothing back, though Eric could tell that the way he had just treated the shit out of his life made him want to get crazy.

"This is what's gon' happen now," Eric said. "You gon' go back out and join lil mama, have you some fun, then you and me we finna take a trip."

"A trip? To where?"

"To the jungle."

T.G. furrowed up. "The jungle?"

"You will be filled in when you get there. Now, go back out there, and I'll see you in a few," Eric said.

"Oh, and one more thing," he added as T.G. quick stepped towards the door.

T.G. paused, half expecting a bullet to hit him.

"If I catch you lookin' at my lady's ass again, I'ma pop yo' snake ass in yours. Now you can go." Eric chuckled to himself as T.G. hurried out. "Bitch ass nigga," he said to himself, then tucked his guns and made his way out to meet back up with his woman.

An Hour Later...

Bunz groaned in frustration. Eric snickered at her.

"What's funny?" she asked him, annoyed by the sounds of love making going on inside the bedroom that had her wishing that she was getting piped down right then.

"The face you makin' right now," Eric told her, taking three steps towards her, closing the gap between them. "You lookin' a little jealous of what's goin' on inside that bedroom right now, baby."

Bunz tried so hard to hide it, but her smile had a mind of its own. She cheezed up so hard that it made Eric chuckle at her again.

"You are a nymphomaniac. Do you know that?" he asked her as the two in the bedroom started sounding like they were going even harder.

"I do. The problem is, what chu' gon' do 'bout it, E? If I'm right, we got about ten to fifteen minutes before we clock back in. So, what's to it, Mr. Problem Solver?"

Eric's hands went to her hips. He looked down into her eyes that seemed to be filled with liquid desire. "I'ma solve your problem," he told her.

Eric unzipped her pants and worked the tight denim material down to her ankles. He kissed her lips sticking his tongue into her mouth exploring her. He heated Bunz up like how the Atlanta weather did when she stepped off of the private jet she flew on from Texas to get there. Her heartbeat raced like a gazelle with a cheetah on its ass. Eric sank down to his knees, kissing her flat stomach on the way. Her womanhood leaked with anticipation, moistening the lace fabric of the tiny Victoria Secret thong she had on. He pulled her right stiletto pump off then pulled her right pants leg off. Bunz lifted her freed leg and rested it on his left shoulder. Eric took her thong's wet center piece between his teeth and yanked it clean off.

"Eric! That was ex—"

"Replaceable. Shut cho' ass up and lemme handle my business, punk," he demanded.

Bunz obeyed with a turned on smile on her face. She licked her lips, eager to feel his lips and tongue work wonders on her. The second she felt Eric French kissing her pussy lips, her knees almost gave out. She bit her lip to keep from moaning out too loudly. It proved to be nearly impossible when Eric started slurping her with his wicked tongue.

"Mmmmm f-f-fuuck! Ooooooo! Eric!" she moaned as quietly as she could.

Eric continued dining on her until he felt her starting to tremble. She was dripping like a water faucet that just wouldn't stop. He hit the brakes on her, stopping right before she could climax. She went to protest until he stood up and silenced her with his wet pussy lips and tongue. Bunz moaned as Eric kissed her. The taste of her own honey on his lips, the fact that they were getting freaky outside the bedroom of a luxurious grand suite that they had managed to slip into, unseen and unheard to finish the last half of one of the most important jobs ever, had Bunz so hot and horny that she was so close to exploding.

The next thing Bunz knew, Eric had slid up inside of her, stretching her out as he filled her up. She wrapped her arms around his neck and held on as he lifted her up and put her against the wall. Eric nailed her as if life depended on her reaching the ultimate *"O"* His hands gripped her ass, her legs wrapped around his waist, his jackhammer pounding her so hard and fast that it made Bunz explode within minutes, all over his dick.

He set her down and hearing that the two in the bedroom were still at it, he made Bunz face the wall, then he entered her from behind. He hit it hard, fast; she bit her lip as the explosive sex had her feeling like she was going to pop. She threw it back at him, adding her own to it. Minutes later, they both came at the same time, while their heartbeats matched each other's.

They then heard the woman in the bedroom cry out the way one did when she orgasmed. Then the man roared as if he had just busted the biggest nut ever.

"Sounds like they're finally done." Bunz chuckled, feeling so much better.

"Hope that nigga got what he needed because where he's going, ain't no guarantee that he's coming back," Eric said retrieving the ripped thong and pocketing it.

Bunz slipped back into her cut-up jeans then put her stilettos back on. Eric stood back at one side of the door, and Bunz stood posted on the other side. Thirty minutes more of waiting, the door finally opened up and out came T.G. He nearly jumped out of his skin when he saw Eric to his left, and peeped Bunz to his right.

"How the hell you get in my spot, nigga?" T.G. demanded to know.

Eric chuckled. "I make things happen, my dude. No more questions. We got a flight to catch."

"To this jungle, right?" T.G. asked with a little more sarcasm than Bunz liked.

"I could have sworn my man said no more questions, nigga!" she snapped wanting to bust his head open with a cast iron skillet.

Again, Eric chuckled. "My lady isn't nice when clowns piss her off, my man. Now let's go. You have only one chance to make your betrayal right, or something really bad is gonna happen to you."

Without another word, T.G. nodded. Like a trained dog that did not want to piss its human off, he followed Eric and Bunz trailed behind him, clutching her knife in her hand, really ready to poke T.G. up if he even looked like he was going to try to run.

Four Hours Later...
"OH SHIT! WAIT, HOLD UP, FAM!" shouted T.G., terrified beyond all reason when the door to the private jet was opened up while it shot through the air like a bullet thousands of feet up over nothing but jungle.

Strapped to an ejectable chair, T.G. held on for dear life as all the pressure behind sucked out of the plane pulled him towards the door.

"Nope! Fuck you, nigga! Get out!" Eric demanded, then holding on himself, he kicked T.G. out of the jet.

"BYE BYE, DICKHEAD!" Bunz shouted out the door right as Eric muscled it back closed.

"Count to ten and hit it bae," he told her.

Bunz groaned. "Do I have to, E? Like, ChaCha 'n' all them are already there. If dude goes splat, JuJu is still gonna get rescued."

Eric chuckled while he shook his head. "Come on, Mo-Mo. Just hit the button, baby."

Bunz groaned with reluctance. She so badly wanted T.G. to die, and there wasn't many better ways for her to be satisfied about it than him smacking the ground at over 100 miles an hour. Instead, she pulled the little remote out of her jeans pocket. She pressed the little button on it. The parachute system that was built into the seat T.G. was plummeting to the ground in, activating, allowing him to land safely, so that the mission awaiting him in Bogota, Colombia could be completed.

Eric stepped over to his woman.

"You dun' turned into a monster since I been gone bae," he said.

Bunz shrugged. "Wait til you see how I become of Trump wins."

He laughed loudly. "Here we go again. I thought you said he's cut from our vocabulary."

"I did, but if we down talk him, then that's okay."

Eric laughed again at his woman. "Baby, on God I love yo' crazy ass."

Bunz frown turned right into a smile. She licked her lips and wrapped her arms around his neck.

"How about you show me how much? We do have about three and a half more hours until we get back to the U.S.

"Not a damn thing would make me happier," Eric told her, then not wasting a second, he scooped his chick up and turned to get her to the bedroom, naked, and up inside her, over and over and over until they touched back down in Atlanta.

Chapter 10

2 Weeks Later...

Tanzania laughed her ass off as the feeling of his tongue lapping up the chocolate sauce and the whipped cream he had splattered and sprayed on her stomach. She shrieked with delight when his tongue dipped down into her belly button, then he kissed it.

"Tiiiim!" she playfully whined as Cardi B's *BODAK YELLOW* bumped from the home audio system, wirelessly connected in Tim's massive bedroom.

"You playin' nigga! Stop teasin' me 'n' give me what I waaant!"

Tim raised his face and looked at her with a playful smirk.

"Shut cho' ass up 'n' lemme do me. I'm in charge tonight, shortie," he told her.

Tanzania pursed her lips together. She tried so hard to keep her smile hidden, but his bedroom blues brought it up out of her.

Tim smiled back at her, then got back to the foreplay. He put his face between her thick thighs and tongue kissed Tanzania's swollen pussy lips like they were the ones on her gorgeous face. She moaned, arching her back as Tim began taking her on another trip to Nirvana. Since they had taken the dive and started dating exclusively, there wasn't a night spent without hot crazy sex, with toe curling foreplay to kick it off, and so many orgasms that Tanzania couldn't remember the name of a single one of her exes. She was really feeling Tim, and he was really feeling her. She had him, and had no plans on letting any other woman get anywhere near him.

Tim flipped her onto her belly and marveled at how phat and plump her ass was. He sprayed a line of whipped cream in between her crack. Tanzania shrieked when she felt the coldness in her crevice then she bit her lip and moaned when she felt his tongue slurp it up. Then suddenly, Tanzania burped loudly. She gasped, covering her mouth with her hand. Her stomach bubbled up. In a flash, she jumped up and ran like a track star towards the bathroom. Tim's eyebrows furrowed with puzzlement. He heard her retching so loudly that it made his skin crawl. Getting up, he headed towards the bathroom.

"Tanz? Are you cool, baby?"

Inside, he saw her on her knees, puking into the toilet. He went to her and kneeled down next to her, rubbing her back. After a few more minutes, her stomach was empty. Tim got her a wet towel and wiped her face for her. Tanzania smiled, appreciating his attentiveness, and the way he catered to her. She could tell he really cared for her. The feelings were definitely mutual.

"You been getting' sick like this every day for the past week, girl. Lemme find out yo' ass got COVID when that shit ain't even relevant anymore," Tim teased.

Tanzania shot him a twisted lip look. "Shut cho' ass up, nigga."

"Uh huh. Don't get to spreadin' that shit to nobody at the bash. Come on, though so we can get fresh and clean."

Tanzania groaned. "I need a Ginger Ale or somethin' bae," she told him as he helped her up from the floor and flushed the toilet for her. "I might just got to sit this one out."

"Maan, heelll naw, Tanzania! Yo, Bunz, and E lost they kids! Now all they got is us, Tracy, LaLa and Deuce. We have to be there; it's Bunz 27th birthday baby."

Though she was still feeling queasy, Tanzania nodded. She opened her mouth to talk, but right before a single syllable out, Tanzania farted loudly, then shrieked, doubling over as her stomach bubbled up.

"Shit! Get out! Get out!" she urged pushing him towards the door.

"Aye, aye, aye! Don't take all night, tryna use this—"

"GET OOOUUT, TIIIM!" she yelled as another fart came out.

She forced him out and slammed the door shut in his face. She ran back to the toilet and plopped down on it right before her bowels evacuated out of control. Tim knocked on the door and hollered out.

"YO ASS BETTER NOT HAVE DROPPED ANYTHING ON MY FLOOR, JOE! WIT'CHO COVID BOOTY HEAD ASS!"

"SHUT THE FUCK UP, TIMOTHY!" Tanzania shouted back, releasing her bowels some more and grunting.

"OPEN A WINDOW WHEN YOU DONE, TOO, LOOSE GUTS!" Tim shouted once more.

Tanzania shook her head. "I'm smack the fuck out of his ass after I wipe my booty. Fuck washin' my hands, too, nigga! Yeah!"

***

Eric's eyes went wide when Bunz emerged from the huge walk-in closet of their massive master bedroom of their new mansion out in the Highland Park area. Looking dazzling in a shimmering long spaghetti strap gown that fell down to her ankles, with her hair, makeup, and nails done, Bunz looked like she was competing for an award. The pointed toe stilettos on her feet looked like they were made of chrome, and the diamond encrusted jewelry she had on dripped so hard.

"Damn!" said Eric dressed in a custom all white three-piece Armani suit, with matching shoes, fresh braids in his head, beard cleaned up, and his own drip flicking as if he was moving.

"You are…wow," he added.

Bunz smiled, feeling very bashful now. "Thank, you baby. I don't think I've ever been dolled up like this before."

"It's yo' birthday, Mo-Mo. You supposed to pop out lookin' like a million dollars."

"Is that how I look?" she asked, doing a slow seductive turn, letting him see all that shiny ass before facing him again. "Like a million dollars?"

"Naw baby. You look better. Like a queen."

Bunz willed herself not to cry. She tried hard, but wishing that their son and daughter were there, instead of in the grave, had her feeling like an emotional roller coaster. Remembering pieces of Andrea in the box had haunted her, but when she began getting little shoe boxes with infant body parts inside, Bunz' heart had broken, shattering to pieces that she couldn't even begin to put back together.

"Hey, hey, baby, no." Eric pulled her into his arms as tears started falling. "Come on, Mo-Mo. Don't cry, baby. Please don't cry."

She buried her face in his chest as she felt his strong arms holding her tightly,

"I miss my babies, E." Bunz wept. "Why them?"

"The Man above works in very mysterious ways, Monique. I'm hurtin' too, but we gotta stay strong. Nothin' can ever hurt them where they are now."

Bunz pulled back and looked up at her man. Her eyes went from grief-stricken to blazing balls of fire in mere seconds.

"I won't rest until that bitch is dead, E. She has to die for what she did, painfully by my hand."

"When she gets stupid and pops up from whatever hole she crawled in, I vow to you, we gon' play 'Whack-A-Mole' with that bitch. On my kids!" he declared as his own emotions started getting away from him.

Bunz reached up and wiped his tears away before they could fall.

"But until that time comes," he continued, "you, me, Tim, Tanzania are gonna live it the fuck up, and anybody that gets in our way will have a closed casket funeral.

"And I'ma shoot the whole funeral home up with everyone inside," Bunz added.

"Let's go celebrate you makin' it to 27 years of life, my love," said Eric, planting a kiss on her lips. "God knows you deserve it, so we finna turn thee fuck up and bring it in together, surrounded by family, friends, and love."

***

Outside of their home, a luxurious Sprinter awaited at the front steps of the stone porch. The big man in a suit and tie that was driving stood at the door waiting to assist them into the spacious vehicle. LaLa and Deuce trotted up to them as Eric and Bunz descended the steps. LaLa, with a big round stomach, wagged her tail excitedly as Eric ruffled her meaty face, kissing her nose.

"Almost time to give birth, huh girl? You gon' be a great mother!" he told her.

Bunz patted Deuce's head.

"Good job boy," she told him, happy for LaLa's pregnancy, though it made her think about when she carried Eric Jr. and Monique for nearly nine months.

"Make sure you keep your eyes on your little ones, Deuce, at all times."

Eric heard his fiancée's words. He knew exactly what she meant.

Leaving the dogs free to roam the expansive yard, or to enter and exit the mansion as they pleased, through a custom-built dog door, Bunz was helped up into the Mercedes mini bus, then Eric joined her. The door was closed. The chauffeur got behind the wheel and pulled off, heading north to get up to Racine, where Bunz' bash was going to be.

***

Arriving at Tim's extravagant and very popular turn-up spot of which he called *Club Racine,* Eric saw how packed the parking lot was. Everything from plain whips, painted up and sat on custom rims to expensive foreign and mullion dollar exotics filled the lot. Eric smiled as he saw how many people had come to show his woman some B-day love.

The chauffeur parked in the front. Two big bouncers opened the door and helped Bunz out. Coming out of the front doors, Tim, Tanzania, followed by Kylie, Cynthia, Amerie, Diedra, Sylvia, and Asia all holding balloons and bouquets of assorted roses and flowers. They had shouted Happy Birthday to Bunz, then the ladies nearly yanked her arm out of socket as they pulled her in.

"Eeeee, yo there is a lot of love up in here tonight! On the Homiez!" Eric heard someone say behind him as he dapped Tim up.

Turning, Eric saw Macho, along with his wife, Yessinia, and G-Baby. All three looked like they were planning to take a stroll down the red carpet to accept the award for the best looking trio of the year. Yessy, Macho's caramel toned Bronx born and raised Nuyorican queen was a stunning 5'9 belle, 33 years of age. Her rich brown hair was braided in the same intricate fishbone design as the braided-up G-Baby. The two curvy Puerto Ricans were dress in custom FeFe Couture mini dresses, stilettos, and dripped diamond jewelry. Macho, himself rocked designer labels and jewelry embedded with flawless diamonds. His line up fresh, razor sharp. His long dreads freshly twisted and in 2-strands hanging loose.

Eric and Tim saw the three had brought the family. Macho's brother Tool, the two younger cousins Javier, Xavier, and Evelyn, whom were all accompanied by their wives and girlfriends. Javi's wife, Michelle stood by her green-eyes super fresh husband. Xavier's wife, a voluptuous woman with fiery red hair that strongly resembled *Wild 'N' Out's* Justina Valentine was there with her husband. Xavier also had his other two baby mommas with him, and even Evelyn, their wild-child baby sister, was present joined by her long-time girlfriend, Gloria.

Behind the thirteen main members of the notorious Valdez family, was Danny Valdez. The man was big. A little shorter than Tool but taller than Macho, and bulky like a body builder. His skin-tone was like brown sugar. His bald fade was fresh, low-trimmed beard lined perfectly, and he rocked designer swag and diamond jewelry. ChaCha was at her husband's side rocking a skin-tight leather Hermes dress with diamond studded Red Bottom pumps. The King and Queen were looking like true royalty in all of its divined splendor. Eric looked at the two and for some reason felt like he was in the presence of the most majestic people on earth.

***

Eric introduced Tim to Macho and his family. Tim had been around Eric for a long time, but he had never actually met any of the Valdez. Up until then, Tim had only heard stories about the big billionaire family. Everything he had heard; he was surprised that their lives hadn't become a movie or that a hood novelist hadn't written a series about them.

"I'm extremely grateful that you all came to help my woman bring in her 27th year of life," Eric told them all. "This is the owner of this fly ass club, my brother from another mother, Tim. He made it so we can all go crazy tonight and not worry about pesky cops or haters."

"That's what the fuck I'm talkin' about cutty!" Macho hollered, taking his women's hands. "Now let's get inside and turn thee fuck up!"

***

Eric and Bunz were treated like celebrities by all. Bunz, especially, was shown so much love that multiple times, she welled up with tears. She hadn't been around so many people that were there for her ever before in her life. She and her fiancé cut loose on the dance floor. Her skills that she acquired in her time as a dancer came back like the muscles on a weightlifter that took a hiatus. Bunz went crazy, shaking what the mother that chose drugs over her gave her. Eric was stuck in a trance, completely amazed. It brought him back to the night he met her at the club she was working at just over three years ago. He was immediately smitten with Bunz. She was gorgeous, exotic, thick, and could clap her ass like she invented twerking.

From that night to everything in between then and now, Eric remembered. He remembered the good, the bad, the ugly, and it instilled such emotions in that he didn't know whether to run to her, pull her to him, and kiss her for coming back to him. Or to run away from her and kill everyone that has so much as disrespected her, let alone did things to her that she allowed as long as they paid.

Paula Paulmatti then popped into his mind. He clenched his teeth and absentmindedly began grinding them. He was furious with himself that he put his dick in her. He cheated on his woman with the woman that tried to kill him, kidnapped his wife, killed Andrea, and his babies. Eric's blood began to boil. He started seeing red. In an instant, he had switched from party mode to beast mode. Just as a bead of sweat ran down his forehead, Eric felt a hand touch his shoulder. He turned around and saw his baby cousin, slightly burned, but still so beautiful. Eric's rage instantly dissipated. Out of all the loss, the return of Tracy had been what had Eric being able to smile. He and Bunz got the call about her being rushed to the ER badly burned. Learning that she had narrowly escaped death via grenades in a closed box truck, through a small window after the twins had been torn from her grasp by Paula Paulmatti's henchmen, Eric and his lady rushed there to be at her side. Tracy was in horrible shape. The doctors and nurses did everything they could and miraculously, Tracy pulled through.

Eric wrapped her up in his arms and hugged Tracy tightly. Tears fell from his eyes onto her head. He had money. He had love. He had businesses, guns, goons, and drugs, but what he barely had was family. Tracy was all he knew that shared his blood and he came so close to losing her. "I love you lil cuz," he told her, trying to get his emotion in check.

"I love you too E," Tracy replied as her own emotions began to go into overdrive. "I'm so sorry. I should've been more aware of my surroundings, cuz."

"Naw, don't put it on yourself, Tracy. The bitch is a slithering snake. She got the upper hand and won. Eric Jr and Monique are gone. We have to deal with it, but there's gonna come a time when—"

BOOM! BOOM! BOOM! BOOM! BOOM!
BRRRR! BRRRR! BRRRRRRRR! BRRRRR!

Eric instinctively grabbed Tracy when gunshots rang out from somewhere in the club. He took her to the floor and immediately looked for Bunz. He saw her being ushered away by Tanzania and the other girls. Five shooters came into his line of sight then. They wore full masks that covered their whole heads, but the way their all-black clothes fit, Eric could tell that they were women.

BOCKA! BOCKA! BOCKA! BOCKA! BOCKA!
BOC! BOC! BOC! BOC! BOC! BOC! BOC!

Eric saw Tim pull out his Sig Saver semi-automatic .357 and got to shooting back. Macho jumped up with a .357 Desert Eagle joining him while the security guards upped and went to start dumping at the shooters. Then a loud crash rocked the club. Eric and Tracy found themselves covered in brick and dust.

"E!" Tim shouted in panic when the old Chevy van crashed into the club pushing right through the wall and crushing a group of people that had unfortunately been unable to escape.

"GO GET HIM! I GOT THESE HOES!" Macho shouted, still dumping at one of the women whom had taken cover behind the DJ stand. Yessy, G-Baby, ChaCha had all stepped up, upping their own semi-autos and popped at the other female gunners while Tool, Danny, Javi, Xavier helped those whom were hit with debris when the wall exploded from the van. Tim ran to help Eric and Tracy up. Thankfully they had just a few scratches.

"WHERE'S BUNZ!" Eric yelled.

"TANZANIA HAS…"

BOC! BOC! BOC!

"AAGHH!"

Tim howled in pain as two slugs slammed into his chest knocking him backwards. Eric and Tracy went into panic mode until he told them he had a vest on.

Turning, Eric looked at the van. Through the shattered windshield he saw another masked shooter behind the wheel. A lock of blonde hair hung from under it. The driver started beeping the horn, shouting to the others. Eric grabbed Tim's gun and started blasting at her. She slammed into reverse and mashed the gas, running over people she'd killed again in her haste to escape bullets flying at her.

Eric and a few of the guards gave chase to the van. They all heard her scream as she whipped a hard left turn, about facing away from the club. Eric ran like he was a track star, dumping the XM17 at the rear of the van. The masked lady slammed it into drive and peeled off, her left hand handing out of the window shooting a 10mm semi-auto.

The gun clicked empty when the last bullet fired. Eric cursed as the van plowed through two parked cars and hopped a grass curb that separated the lot from the small highway road that ran next to it. He watched the van speed west up Highway 20 until the taillights were tiny specs in the distance.

Running back to the club, Macho and Tool helped Tim up. Bunz, Tanzania, the others, along with Yessy, G-Baby, and ChaCha had laid out all but one of the shooters. The one that remained alive trembled in fear as Yessy's .44 Bulldog touched the back of her head. Eric swallowed his woman up in his arms. He thanked the Man above that she was safe. He glanced at where nine people lay dead from the van hitting them. Eric grinded his teeth, irate that someone had the audacity to shoot up his woman's bash.

He walked up to the shooter chick and snatched her mask off. The girl was young, too young with raven-black hair and blue eyes that were red and filled with tears.

"Who had you do this and bitch if you lie, I will peel yo' muthafuckin' skin off while you're still alive!" Eric threatened.

She managed to sneak her hand into her pocket. By the time anyone realized it, she had her hand back out and quickly put something in her mouth.

"What the fuck was that?" demanded Yessy, ramming the barrel of her revolver into the girl's head, thumbing the hammer back,

She hit the floor. Seconds later, she started shaking, trembling, convulsing. She foamed at the mouth, her body seizing up. Eric, Bunz, Tim, and the others watched as the girl soon took her last breath. Her body went limp and something green leaked from the side of her lips.

"This bitch just poisoned herself yo!" Macho exclaimed with furrowed brows.

"What in the actual fuck?" Bunz said to herself. "Why would she do that? She was just a little girl!"

"Like the rest of them," Tim added.

"I've seen this before; cyanide pills for when someone who works for someone else fucks up a mission and has to take the easy way out as punishment or suffer the wrath of who they was carryin' out the hit for," Eric said turning from looking at the dead girl to his woman.

"The question is who the hell put such fear in her that she actually went through with it?"

"It has to be Paula, baby! It has to be!" Bunz said.

"Paula fled the country," Yessy chimed in. "Not sayin' she couldn't do this by a simple call, but for some reason, I feel like it's someone else."

Eric and Bunz exchanged glances with each other, curious as to who else could be gunning for them, that actually had the means to get close.

"I know one thing," Tim said as Tanzania helped remove the damaged bullet proof vest. "When I get my hands on whoever that was drivin' the van, on erthang I love, I'm light her ass on fire and let her run out into the middle of a busy highway for shootin' me."

Chapter 11

Paula laughed her ass off when she was informed of what came about when her protégé went on her very first solo mission.

"It's not funny. All those little girls," the chick said sounding very upset about it. "Not a single one of them were over 15 years old, Paula!"

"You sound like you still have a heart. I thought I helped you get rid of it?" Paula asked.

She heard the girl smack her lips.

"You can't get rid of having a heart. Even you still have one, twisted bitch or not. If your damn boyfriend was still here, you'd be beggin' him to wife you."

Paula's smile then turned into a frown.

"Look, you ungrateful whore, get the fucking job done, or I will kill you! Look at what happened to you! You're gonna let that bitch live! She lied to you! Lies are punishable by death! KILL HER!"

Paula ended the call, slamming her phone down on the table next to her.

"Okay, I'm done; you can finish," she said looking down at Dominic.

He smiled up at her through her parted legs. On his knees in front of her, in the lavish and spacious living room of her big villa, just outside of Milan, Dominic had the Paulmatti princess all to himself with no one to interrupt.

"With pleasure, ma'am." The head security guard as Paula now called him got back to orally pleasing her as he'd yearned to do when he first laid eyes on the Paulmatti princess.

Paula closed her eyes and bit her bottom lip, as she enjoyed the feeling the muscular Italians lips and tongue working her clit gave her.

"Mmmm yeeeeaah... it feels so good to be the most untouchable bitch in the world...and maaan, this motherfucker can suck pussy! WOOO!"

***

A few hours after Tim's club crawled with cops, detectives and crime scene techs, the bodies were carted off by the coroners, and the club was boarded by the city workers, commissioned by the Racine Police Chief. Everyone left saddened by the devastating night that was supposed to be special for Bunz. The Valdez posse was the last of the guests to leave, but not until they were sure Eric and Bunz were safe as well as Tim, his lady Tanzania, and the others. They climbed up into the multi-million-dollar coach bus they pulled up in and rode off.

Eric and Bunz got back into the Sprinter and headed off to somewhere else, unwilling to allow bullets to blow their night. The ladies and the fellas all left. Tim and Tanzania were last.

"Lemme drive bae," she told him holding her hand out for the key to his new Corvette Stingray Z51 convertible.

"Heeell no."

"Come oooon, Tim! You just got shot! Let a bitch take care of her man!"

"No," Tim again declined, hitting the unlock button on the fob. "You feel the need to take care of a nigga, then wait until we get home.

Tanzania pouted but refrained from arguing further. At the passenger's side, she slid herself down into the black leather interior, holding the hem of her super-short mini dress down as it tried to ride up her thighs. Tim closed the door and hopped behind the wheel. He started the engine up, catching goose bumps from the sound. Putting the push button automatic transmission in drive, Tim hit the gas and peeled off making use of the 650 horsepower the Ferrari looking Vette came off the lot with.

Tanzania looked over at her man and smiled. Any nigga that took bullets even with a bulletproof vest on and still looked that handsome was the type for her. The way he cruised with one arm on the wheel, nodding his head to YFN Lucci and Plies *IN A MINUTE* had naughty thoughts swimming around in her head. Her pussy started tingling with arousal, nipples getting hard, yearning for his lips and tongue work. Unable to wait until they got to his home, Tanzania wanted to get the party started a little early. She clicked off her seatbelt and got up on her knees in the seat.

"What is you...?" Tim began to ask as she reached over to his crotch and started to undo his pants.

"Don't ask no dumb questions, nigga," Tanzania told him, freeing his 9 inches of hardness. "Just drive us home, and while you do that, I'ma keep this ready to beat this pussy up like you wish you could do to whoever was drivin' that van."

She lowered her head down, mouth wide open, and engulfed him, going balls deep. Tim groaned gutturally. Her mouth was so warm and wet. It made him swerve a little like he was tipsy. Tanzania tooted her ass up high and deep throated Tim's dick like a pro. Tim did his best to focus on the nearly deserted road ahead of him, but her head game had both of his feet tap dancing like they had a mind of their own.

"Gooooddaaamn!" he cursed when she started sucking him faster, adding one of her hands and jerking him.

Tanzania was going bananas. She wanted to make him nut so hard that he sneezed. She lifted up and sucked on the bulbous tip, swirling her tongue around it. Releasing him, she spit on it. She turned her head and looked up at him with cum on her chin. Tim glanced down at her, seeing the sexiest dick sucking face ever right before she took his hand and sucked on his middle finger, getting it wet. Tim took the hint and when she let his finger to inhale his dick back into her mouth, he reached his hand around her backside, raised her tiny dress up, exposing her juicy ass.

It was looking like a sweet-sour apple gumball in the green fishnet pantyhose she'd chosen to wear with the white and green Gucci monogrammed dress and white pumps to go with it. He smacked her ass before stuffing his finger through one of the fishnet holes at her crack. Tanzania welcomed his finger into her asshole, moaning as he started finger fucking it. She let go of his shaft and sucked with no hands, head bobbing up and down in his lap as fast as a punk rock lover listening to their favorite song off the powder.

Tim was glad to see they were coming to a traffic light. He was so close to busting his nut and wanted to enjoy it without worrying about hitting anything. At the intersection that sat right before Interstate 94, surrounded by 18-wheeler truck stops, restaurants, and hotels, Tim brought his C8 to a stop and hurried to push the park button.

"Oh shit! Shit! Fuck! I f-f-finna buss! Ooohhh sssshhhit!" he hollered as Tanzanina went harder.

Right as he felt it rising to the tip, Tim heard tires screeching. He opened his eyes and saw the same van that had ran into his club on his passenger's side with the masked driver pointing a Glock at him and Tanzania.

"TANZ!" Tim shouted as she rose up from his lap.

She just managed to turn her head to see behind her when the driver opened fire.

BOC! BOC! BOC!

"AAAAAAAAAHHHHHH!" Tanzania screamed when three hollow points flew into her ass.

Tim mashed the gas pedal but went nowhere, as it was still in park. The masked shooter laughed then she hit the gas peeling off.

"TANZ! NO!" Tim panicked seeing she was unconscious. "FUUUCK!"

The van had disappeared once it hopped onto the highway, shooting north. Tim wasted no time. He hit drive and mashed the gas, peeling off in a rush to get to the ER before Tanzania bled to death.

"Hold on, baby! Hold on!" he told her, yanking it to the left to hop onto southbound 94, aiming to get to Kenosha's Emergency Medical Center.

"I can't lose you too, Tanzania! Please hold on!"

Tim sailed past the very few bits of traffic on the highway, pushing his Vette past 160 miles an hour. In minutes, he got to Route 60 and hopped off the highway, then in less than twenty seconds skidded to a stop in the E.R. zone. He jumped out and ran in screaming for help. He got a few nurses' attention. They rushed out with a stretcher and got Tanzania on it then they hauled ass to get her to surgery.

Tim made it only to the O.R. hallway doors before one of the nurses stopped him. He stood there, tears falling, anger soaring out of control. He marched back outside to his car and grabbed his phone making a call to the only person he could call for help, while hoping to not ruin Bunz birthday any more than it had already been.

***

Boarding the private jet at the private airport in Kenosha, Bunz and Eric got comfortable in the luxurious confines of the Lear jet. The captain announced they were cleared for takeoff, minutes later. After it taxied to the runway and took off, levelling out just above 30,000 feet, the flight attendant brought a chilled bottle of Moet with two crystal champagne flutes. She popped the bottle with a smile. Then, she poured Bunz up. Then Eric. She wished Bunz a Happy Birthday then took her leave to give the two their privacy.

Bunz looked over at where Lala laid stretched out on her side, her belly protruding filled with baby Bullies. Deuce was laid out by her side, his head resting on her shoulders. He was smiling at the sight of male and female harmony that would kill for each other and die for each other. Eric knew what his woman was thinking as she looked at the dogs. He only wished that he and Bunz were more like Lala and Deuce; blessed with their pups and living a ride or die life to the end of time. Then he smiled himself knowing that besides their pups being taken away from them, he and Bunz were living a ride or die life, and no matter what, Eric refused to ever let anything come between them again.

"Bae," he called to her.

Bunz looked at him.

"Yes, my handsome King?"

"Come here. Lemme talk to you real quick, my beautiful queen."

She got up from her seat and took her place on his lap, sitting sideways. Looking down into his soulful eyes, Bunz smiled, feeling her heart swell up in her chest. His eyes did something to her that she just could not understand. Everything about him made her so incredibly happy. He was her rock, and she was his air. He protected her, and she protected him. Neither of them feared death but losing each other was something that would be one hundred times worse than taking their last breath.

"I wanna marry you, Monique," Eric told her looking up into her glistening eyes.

She held up her finger showing him the 8-carat diamond engagement ring on her finger that he put there.

"I think you made that clear, E," Bunz chuckled.

"Naw, baby. I mean as soon as we touch down. Let's just do it. Let's get married tonight."

"But what about Tracy and Tim?" she asked, linking her finger around his, both of them with matching tattoos, hers saying *Forever His Queen,* and his saying *"Forever Her King,"* while over their hearts, they had *"M&E 4Ever"* inked.

"They'll be okay. I'm tryna make you Mrs. Bounds to-motherfuckin'-night, baby. What do you say?"

Bunz smile turned into a huge pearly white grin. She nodded her head, cupping his face with her hands.

"Yes. Let's do it, Eric," she agreed.

Bunz leaned down and planted a passionate kiss on his lips. Instantly, sparks of fireworks went off between them as their souls met and became one. Then a minute later, they were both naked.

***

She ran into the ER entrance and saw him sitting in the waiting area, looking horrible. His eyes were red, face tight, and he had blood on him. He was stuck, frozen, staring at the floor. He didn't even hear Tracy stopping at his side and crouched down. She took Tim's hand into hers. He came back when he felt her. He looked at her. Tracy let his hand go and put her arms around him. Tim broke down then, sobbing into her shoulder.

"I'm here, Tim. I got you, fam," Tracy assured him, as her own eyes welled up with tears.

"Who the fuck is this bitch, Tracy! And why the fuck is she at us?" Tim pleaded to know.

Tracy shook her head.

"I wish I knew, babe. I swear I do, but you know as well as I do…the enemy is always revealed because the enemy always makes a mistake. We will find out and the bitch is gon' beg for death because of the pain she gon' feel. That's on my momma, fam."

Tim nodded his head against her shoulder and raised his head.

"Hit Chief up. Maybe he can help us find the van," Tim suggested then.

Tracy nodded and got her phone out so she could hit up Eric's plug in the Racine Police Department. The man had been a true asset to the team thus far. Now it was time to put him back to work to find a drop of water in the Atlantic Ocean with absolutely nothing to go off.

***

A few hours later, into the early morning, the jet touched down at Miami International. Eric and Bunz both back dressed, got ready to deboard. LaLa and Deuce stretched their legs and went by the door, anxious to get out. They could sense that they were not in the Midwest anymore. The flight attendant, the captain, and the assistant pilot stood at the bottom of the steps. They all smiled at their passengers and the dogs as they descended the stairway.

Pulling up was an exclusive long wheelbase Phantom, rolling on white 24-inch Forgiatos that matched the big car. It came to a stop by where Eric, Bunz, and their dogs sat. The driver got out and nodded with a smile. He introduced himself as Raul and opened the rear suicide door. Bunz got in, Eric after her, then the dogs. The driver got back behind the wheel and took them to South Beach, where the recently renovated 5-stay tall loft building sat across from Miami's most popular beach. Bunz, Eric, the dogs, all got out thanking their driver, whom informed them that he was at their service for the duration of their stay. He handed them his card then headed off.

Inside the building's main loft, vintage Miami décor made one feel as if they had gone back into times when men in fancy suits with gold chains around their necks, Ray Bans on their faces, and loafers on their feet, bring in kilos of cocaine on expensive cigarette boats.

"Love what you did to the place bae," Eric said remembering how it looked when Bunz first brought it after getting a 165 million dollar pay day from selling a vintage diamond necklace and a bunch of rare colored diamonds to Eric's diamond connoisseur and play sister Soniya. The jewels came from an Italian mobster diamond jeweler that Bunz murdered, who was none other than Paula Paulmatti's father.

Bunz smiled. It still smelled fresh inside, like the ocean and clean air.

"I haven't been here since..." She paused as she was about to say since he died.

Eric went to her, took her hand, and led her towards the big glass retracting doors to the spacious patio deck. LaLa and Deuce followed sniffing around exploring the unfamiliar place.

Outside in the cook misty early morning, Eric brought his woman to the railing. The view of South Beach Blvd., and the beach across the famous street put a smile on Bunz's face. Eric wrapped his arms around her and held her from behind. He laid his chin on her shoulder. Bunz reached a hand back and stroked his chin lovingly. She regained her sense of peace by the feeling of him behind her, his arms around her, and his magic stick pressed against her ass, growing harder and harder by the second.

"I love you, Monique," Eric said into her left ear.

Bunz turned around. She wrapped her arms around his neck and smiled at him.

"And I love you Eric," Bunz replied back with love in her eyes. "Make love to me baby. Right now."

Eric grinned. "With pleasure, my queen," he told her and, in an instant, had the suede ties at the sides of her shimmering ensemble untied.

Her dress fell to the floor. No bra, no panties, Bunz stood before her man in her birthday suit looking like the sweetest piece of caramel candy a man could get his hands on. Eric licked his lips at the thick deliciousness in front of him. Less than ten seconds later, he was out of his clothes dick bone hard and pointing at what it was dying to dive into. Bunz bit her lip at the sight of chiseled perfection. Her pussy dripped down her thighs as she grew so hot for him.

He stepped up to her, wrapped her in his strong arms, kissed her, his hardness pressing against her wetness. Eric backed her to the long couch on the patio picking her up. Bunz wrapped her legs around him. He sat down with her on his lap, and seconds later, she slid down on his length. Eyes locked onto each other, they made love with their bodies and their souls all the way until the sun rose up. They ended up in the big king-size bed up on the spacious upper loft, passing out sweaty and satisfied.

Chapter 12

Paula giggles at herself as she looked in her full-body mirror. Bending over, she made her perky little ass wiggle. She dressed for the multiple special occasions for the day. Glamorously, she dolled herself up, wanting to show the prissy bitches of Milan who the real beauty queen was. The skin-tight Versace dress she clothed herself in did just that, with its royal ultraviolet purple color, gold embroidering, open back design, The long-sleeved top half was sheer, see through; her gold bra concealed her breasts. The bottom mid-thigh length half was leather, with a slit up the front allowing her upper thighs to be seen when she took a step. Her legs were freshly waxed and oiled, glistening from the light in her bedroom. Down on her feet, the 6-inch YSL pumps she rocked matched the gold metallic lipstick she wore and the eyeshadow. Her hair was flat ironed. She smelled like lavender.

"Mirror, mirror on my wall, tell these Milan bitches that Paula Paulmatti is thee baddest bitch of them all," she said to herself, then she blew herself a kiss.

Paula went to get the rare purple and yellow-gold necklace that went with her earrings in her ears from around the little flat box on her bed when a knock at her double doors halted her.

"Madam Paulmatti?" the tall olive-toned butler said as he cracked open one of the doors.

"Your vehicle awaits you."

"Come in, Horatio," Paula told him as she took the necklace out of its box.

6 feet, 4 inches of olive-tone Italian in a custom suit entered. Paula looked at him. His hair slicked back, face freshly shaved, his eyes blue like the Caribbean Sea waters.

"Help me put this on," Paula told him. "And close the door."

Horatio nodded and obeyed. He closed the door and went to her. She turned her back to him and let him put on the 8.5-million-dollar necklace.

"There," he said taking a step back.

Paula turned back to him and struck a pose.

"How do I look, Horatio?"

"Stunning, Ms. Paulmatti. Absolutely Bellissima!" he said lusting for the beautiful mob princess so hard.

She smiled at him then. "Do you find me attractive, Horatio?"

"Uh…" he hesitated to answer her question.

She laughed. "Don't be scared. You're too big for that shit, dude."

Horatio felt his manhood being challenged. He stepped closer to her, getting an even stronger whiff of the mouth-watering perfume she had on.

"I am very attractive to you madam," he told her standing half a foot away.

Paula licked her lips at him. "Would you fuck me, Horatio?" she then asked looking up into his eyes.

"All over Italy, madam."

She closed the gap between them and reached her hand out to grab his crotch. Her eyes went wide when she felt the big bulge. Horatio gave her a seductive smirk seeing in her facial expression that she was loving what she was feeling. Paula let it go and went to undo his trousers.

"Madam your driver—"

"Fuck the driver!" she snapped, cutting him off as she yanked his pants and underwear down, freeing his thick hardness.

"I get what I want when I want it! And right now, I want to suck your cock! So shut the fuck up and put it in my mouth!"

Paula fell to her knees and opened her mouth wide. Horatio's dick swelled even more at how delicious her lips looked. He did exactly as she asked, grabbing his dick at the base and put it right in her mouth. She stuck her tongue out so she could fit all 8 inches down her throat. She gagged as his huge size stretched her esophagus out. He took her head between his hands and started fucking her mouth. Paula's womanhood leaked as she grew even more aroused from the feeling of his balls slapping against her chin over and over again. He grunted, cursed, and groaned. Paula felt like a dirty little whore. She loved it when a man could make her feel like that.

Horatio's cock spasmed in her mouth. She tasted the little bit of pre-cum that was coming out. She made him let her head go, took his dick out of her mouth, and spit a wad of saliva pre-cum onto the head. Looking up at him, Paula slurped it all back up, swallowed, and got back to it, using one of her hands to jerk him while she sucked. He groaned when she used her other hand to cup and massage his balls. Feeling his nut coming, Horatio announced he was close. Paula released him and demanded that he cum all over her face. Horatio was too happy to do so. He grabbed his joint and jerked it hard and fast, howling and cursing as he skeeted hot globs of semen all over her face. She stuck her tongue out catching plenty of it. She swallowed, then she licked his dick clean.

"Wow. That was great!" he exclaimed.

"Lick my face clean, Horatio," Paula requested still on her knees.

Horatio's eyes went wide in shock.

"C-Come again?"

"I said lick your cum off my face! Now!"

He immediately went speechless. Her freakiness turned into creepiness in the blink of an eye.

"Madam you are telling me to—"

"DOMINIC! SOMEBODY HEEEELP! RAAAAPE!"

Horatio gasped. He started backing away as Paula continued screaming for help, staying positioned on her knees. Seconds later, right as Horatio contemplated making a run for it, the double doors to Paula's bedroom flew open. Dominic and five of his men ran in and immediately saw her on her knees with cum all over her face and Horatio backing towards the big window.

"GET HIM!" Paula screamed.

"NO! SHE'S LYING!" Horatio panicked, terrified.

Dominic pulled out his Berretta and cocked it. His other men upped their pistols and pointed at Horatio.

"Dominic! Please! She wanted—"

BOCKA!

Dominic shot Horatio right between his legs. Paula grinned evilly, listening to the man scream so high pitched that a few of Dominic's men had to cover their ears.

BOCKA!

Dominic fired again, hitting Horatio in his chest, then popped him six more times, puting the last two in his face. He hurried over to Paula who had put her fake tears back to work while his men got to work to remove the dead butler.

"I don't know why he did this to me!" she cried. "I begged him to stop, Dom! I swear baby!"

Pulling her up from the floor, Dominic rushed her to the bathroom and washed her face off. Paula wrapped her arms around him, hugging him tightly.

"I will never let another man touch you again, my love. You are mine. I will protect you," Dominic proclaimed.

Paula buried her face in his sternum hiding the demented smile that she could not stop from forming.

"UNTOUCHABLE QUEEN BITCH! YEAH! HAA!" She clowned inside of her head feeling the high-octane rush fill her from being the most conniving rich bitch on the planet that had every man that liked pussy trying to get him some her.

Days Later...

Tim smiled, feeling his heart pound in his chest. She had him wowed and amazed, hypnotized by her lips, her thighs. She stood before him ass naked wearing his name above her right breast in blue ink. Her fiery red hair flowed like a mane made of flames. She was hot, begging for his touch. Tim got up off the bed naked like her, and walked to her, dick swinging as he grew harder. Music serenaded them; the sounds of Wayne Wonder's hit song *NO LETTING GO* flowed through the speakers around the luxuriant confines of his master bedroom. The mood was just right. He was ready for her, and she was ready for him.

Tim stepped up to her, dwarfing her by at least five inches. He lifted her chin up with a finger. She gazed into his eyes and smiled.

"Tell me how bad you want it, baby," he told her speaking in such a deep and low tone that it gave her goosebumps.

"I want it really bad, Tim," she told him, begging and purring at the same time. "Give it to me, daddy. Punish me!"

He scooped her up off of her feet. He took her to his bed, and laid her down, then climbed on top. Kissing her lips, moving down her body, sucking her breasts, kissing her flat stomach, he opened her legs wide and put his face in between them. She hissed, moaned, bit her bottom lip as he sucked on her clit. He was loud about it, sloppy, wild, just like he knew she liked. The way her back arched up off of the bed, the way she squealed and cried out at the top of her lungs, and the way she just kept leaking like a broken faucet told him that he was indeed putting it down.

"Tim! Oohh God, Tim! Shit! Yes!" she cried feeling her climax coming on strong.

Tim went harder, slurping and sucking the shit out of her pussy, making her go bananas. Ten seconds later, he was smacked in the face with hot juices that exploded from deep inside of her. He licked her all up, relishing the taste of her nectar. He kissed her slick pussy lips, smiling at it, then he lifted himself up ready to slide up in it.

"What the fuck!"

Tim froze when he pulled his face up from between her legs not expecting to be looking down the barrel of a Glock.

"You cheating bastard! Fuck you!" she snapped, eyes suddenly full of rage and hatred.

"A-Andrea! You tweakin' right now, joe!" he said jumping back. "Put the gun up, bae!"

BOC!

"AAHHH!"

The bullet hit him in his stomach knocking him backwards. He flew back against the wall.

BOC!

She fired again, missing this shot. She jumped up off of the bed as Tim tried to crawl away, leaving a bloody trail on the floor. She caught him, forced him to roll over, then stood right over him pointing the gun right at the center of his face.

"You were supposed to protect me, Tim!" she sobbed, her hands trembling with a finger wrapped around the trigger.

"I wasn't there when the bitch took you, Drea! You know that!"

She shook her head.

"You let her! You fucking let her!"

"Andrea! Baby please!"

"NO! PLEASE NOTHING! ROT IN HELL YOU PIECE OF BLUE EYED SHIT!" she screamed.

Then she pulled the trigger.

BOC!

"NO!"

Tim jumped out of his sleep, snatching at his FN and pointing it, but there was nobody in front of him, only a big 55-inch HDTV mounted on the retracting ceiling stand. The sounds of beeping from the heart monitor is all he heard. It was dark outside. The curtains were open, the windows too, allowing a cool breeze to flow through the hospital room.

Tanzania, still unconscious was laid out face down, hanging suspended from a doctor made contraption to keep her off of her injured rear. The surgery went well, but having fallen into a coma, the doctors had no clue when she would come to. Tim hadn't left her side in four days. His phone was shut off. He knew Eric and Bunz had likely been calling him like crazy. Probably had people looking for them. He was too distraught to care at the moment. Tanzania was lying in a comatose state, and he would bet every last dollar of his that it was because of him. He looked over at her. Seeing her like that had him feeling horrible. He stood and took her hand.

"I'll be back, baby. I promise," he told her.

Grabbing his phone, Tim left out of the room to head out. He couldn't stay there right now. It hurt too much to see her that way, so he decided to make a few runs and get on top of things, like he'd been chosen by Eric and Bunz to do.

***

Dominic cursed as he exploded. Paula swallowed it all and sat back upright in the passenger's seat of the rare Pagani Huayra Roadster. She giggled to herself at the look on his face while he tried to get his limo cock tucked back into his pants before they pulled up to the big castle like structure where the diamond show was taking place. Behind them, four SUVs with Dominic's men trailed keeping their eyes open and their European built semi-autos close by. They had strict orders to shoot first, fuck asking questions, if anyone got too close to Paula that even remotely seemed like a threat.

Pulling up to what looked like a giant brick castle, Paula saw so many Ferraris, Lamborghinis, and Bugatti's there that she swore that Enzo, Ferruccio, and Ettore were throwing a party. She grew excited knowing there was some serious money inside, money that she planned on taking and adding to the rest of her bank accounts.

"It's going to be a beautiful night, my love," Dominic said pulling up to where valet drivers awaited to take guests' vehicles and park them.

"Indeed, it is handsome," Paula replied with a smirk on her face.

The security guards that were positioned with the valet workers hurried to assist Paula out of the exotic hyper car. Dominic popped the hood which was really the trunk and got the two leather boxes out. Giving them to Paula, he waited for his team to step up. His men hopped out of the two SUVs with their weapons concealed inside their full-length trench coats. They followed Dominic as he led the way inside of the exclusive Palazzo Parigi Hotel & Grand Spa Milano.

***

So many people were inside. It was like a huge gala, full of impeccably dressed men and women, draped in diamond jewelry. Armed security was all over, looking more like secret service operatives. Opera music played from a live orchestra. Waiters and waitresses walked around carrying

big silver plates with flutes of champagne and hors
d'oeuvres.

Paula was greeted by many people that knew her father.
Other mob members, businessmen and women, entrepreneurs,
and wannabes were present. She plastered on a smile as she
shook hands with more people than she cared to hear a word
from.

"Kiss ass motherfuckers," she thought to herself wanting
to smack the shit out of the next person claiming to express
their condolences for the loss of her father and her mother.

"Don't you hate it when people kiss ass?"

Paula laughed then glanced to her right. She saw two
amazingly gorgeous women in stunning diamond studded
dresses with diamonds around their necks, hanging from
their ears, around their wrists and fingers. One was tall as
hell with creamy light butter pecan brown skin, long silky
brunette hair, and the most piercing artic blue eyes Paula had
ever seen. Her sleeveless ensemble allowed her tattooed
arms to show. She had so many that Paula felt a little
intimated.

The second woman was the color of brown sugar with her
honey gold shoulder length hair in perfect spirals. She was
much shorter than the Amazon tall goddess, but equal in
height to the 5'5" tall Paula. Amazed by the two ladies, Paula
couldn't help but to stare at them. They were like royal
stallions, exotic beauties to say the least. Just then, two men
walked up and handed the two women flutes if bubbly. Paula
looked at the big brown skinned giant with broad shoulders,
a clean bald-faded haircut, and a beard so sharply lined that
it looked tattooed on. She surmised he was at least 6'4" tall,
towering over the Amazon chick.

The other man, golden brown skinned with a fresh fade
hypnotizing green eyes, and a sharp beard as well, towering
over the spiral haired woman caught Paula's eye like a horny
slut seeing real love at first sight.

"Holy shit! Goddamn he's fine!" she thought to herself wanting to fan herself as it seemed to have gotten hotter.

"Yeah," Paula said, finding the will to take her eyes off of the green-eyes heart throb. "Too much of that's going on, and I just got here."

"I love that necklace you're wearing," the tall woman told her. "I have a few that are just like it."

"A few? No way this giant bitch has these diamonds on multiple necklaces!" Paula told herself.

"Thanks...um...I'm Paulina, Paula for short. Who are you?"

"Athena, and this is my husband Luis; the other two are our little cousins, Guapa and Veronica."

Paula nodded her head acknowledging the others, then turned back to the tower with breasts.

"So, you say you have a few of these? That must've been expensive to acquire."

The woman chuckled.

"I have a lot of businesses that afford me such things, but they were purchased by my loving husband."

Paula looked at him.

"And what field of work are you in?"

He gave her a shrug, a light shrug.

"A little of this and a little of that."

"Oh. Okay. Right." Paula went back to the tall belle. "Who did you get yours from?"

"Karma."

"I buy from her too! I just never met, nor have I ever seen her. But her diamonds are some of the most precious and faultless out there."

"I only deal with the best, said the spiral haired chick.

Paula turned to her with a puzzled expression etched on her face. The woman smiled at her.

"Nice to finally meet you," she said then.

"You're Karma?" Paula gasped.

"In the flesh," Green eyes spoke up. "My wife prefers people to see her diamonds and custom jewelry, rather than her beautiful smile."

"Ay, Dios mi, escucha a mi sexy marido hablo esa 'mielda," his wife said with a smile.

Paula's eyebrows furrowed up. She hadn't expected the woman to be bilingual. She looked Black, as did her husband, and the big guy. The tower with boobs looked like she could be from Spain.

"Well, it was nice to meet you, Paula," the tall woman said. "See you around."

The four left and disappeared into the thick crowd of people. Paula stood there, feeling like she had just been in the presence of some very powerful people. It was like they radiated importance.

"Dominic?" she called, snapping her finger.

"Yes?" he said, stepping next to her.

"Find out who those people are. They definitely somebodies and I want to know who, now!"

"Yes, ma'am," Dominic replied.

He gave the order to one of his men and stepped back in place as her head security guard. Paula caught sight of the man with the emerald eyes again, smiling down at his wife before leaning in to kiss her.

"You wanna kiss something, huh? I got somethin' real sweet for those lips, Guapo," she thought as her nymphomaniac mind shifted into overdrive and mashed the gas.

"Are you okay? You been staring at that guy for two minutes now," she heard Dominic say to her.

"Mind your business dude," Paula replied waving him off, still with her fantasy in her line of sight, soon to be come her next conquest.

Chapter 13

Eric grinded his teeth in anger, as he listened to Tim tell him about what happened to Tanzania. He was already pissed that his top dog had been unreachable for days, and how Tracy had been hesitant to say as to why. Money poured into his and Bunz's accounts from their dope spots and their businesses, but Eric could care less about money when it came to the wellbeing of his people.

"You and me finna have a talk about you feelin'. It's okay to fall off the face of the earth, then up and hit my line and think I'm not gon' be on one," Eric told him. "Where's Tracy at?"

"Meetin' with the people for the new location of the salon and boutique. I'm 'bout to make a big deposit then I'm ..."

Eric's eyebrows furrowed.

"You're what?"

"Hold up, bro. I swear I keep seein' the same Audi everywhere I go," Tim said.

"What does yo' instincts tell you, Tim?" Eric asked, annoyed that the young, seasoned underboss still questioned strange occurrences.

"To handle it," Tim answered.

"Handle it then, bruh. When you get done, go get Tracy and y'all get to Miami ASAP. Bunz and I got something we tryna show you."

He heard Tim groan then.

"Chill out, bruh. We ain't finna get on y'all bumper. Just fly down."

"Aight. We'll be down, my nigga."

Eric ended the call then, shaking his head. Sitting on a lounge chair on the sand, he saw Bunz playing with Deuce in the water. LaLa was laying by Eric's feet, resting her pregnant body. His iPhone dinged as Deuce jumped his almost 200-pound body nearly five feet in the air to catch a frisbee. Chuckling at the cheers and laughter from others taking a day off from life on South Beach, Eric looked at his phone and saw he had a message. He opened it and viewed it. Finishing it, Eric smirked to himself. After sending a thumbs up emoji, he set his phone back down and continued watching his wife and dog enjoy some well-deserved fun in the sun.

***

Tim whipped his white-on-white Range Rover Supercharged into the alley way and floored it until it reached a space between two garages to turn in and post for a minute. He turned his lights off, grabbed his Desert Eagle, cocked it, waiting in the dark. He could see headlights seconds later. With his hand on the handle to the door, eagerly he got ready. The little silver Audi A5 appeared, rolling slowly. Tim couldn't see inside despite the bright lights in the alley. The windows were tinted too darkly. The car rolled up to the rear of Tim's Range rover. The driver stopped right behind it. Tim jumped out and ran towards it, gun up, finger around the trigger. Teeth gritted; he aimed at the car's passenger window. The engine revved up, then the rear wheels screeched as the driver mashed the gas. Tim jumped out into the middle of the alley and pointed at the rear window, closing one eye; honing in on the driver's side. *BOOM! BOOM! BOOM! BOOM! BOOM! BOOM!* He squeezed six shots out. The back window exploded. He heard a scream, then the car lost control and went head into a garage. Tim ran back to his Range, hopped in, backed out of the spot, and sped up to the crashed Audi. Pulling up next to it, he saw the driver through the busted-out windows. It was a young guy, a white boy.

He hopped out and pointed his gun at the guy's head through the passenger's window. The driver looked at him with blood dripping down his face from the gash on his forehead.

"Who has you followin' me and why? Lie once, and you die forever," Tim declared.

The guy dug in his pocket and hurried to pull out what he had in it. Tim watched him pop something into his mouth and swallow.

"Maaan, come on joe! Again, with these poison pills!"

The tailer immediately started convulsing, foaming at the mouth like he was overdosing. Tim stepped back as the man took his last breath.

"This shit is crazy, fam! Fuck is wrong with these dumbass white people?" he asked himself incredulously, jumping back into his SUV and dipping out the alley.

Hurrying from the K-Town neighborhood, Tim made it safely through the west side to the expressway and hopped on. Traveling north with the steady flow of traffic, he took a deep breath once he felt like he had gotten far enough away. Grabbing his iPhone, he called Tracy.

"Yeah, what up, fam?"

"Tracy, E wants us down in Miami ASAP. Finish up you doin' and meet me at yo' crib."

"Everything cool?"

116

"I have no clue, but white people keep killin' themselves. I'll explain when I get to you."

"Ride safe. See you soon, fam," Tracy replied, then ended the call.

Tim readjusted himself in his seat and took another deep breath, trying to calm his nerves. He turned the music on and let the sounds of YFN Lucci and Latto talking about wet pussy ease his mind.

***

Sitting at her table, surrounded by Dominic's men, Paula watched green eyes, and his wife mingle with people in the crowd. The other two were speaking with another couple, laughing loudly at whatever joke was being said. She felt so envious of the four. They had love, something that Paula so badly wanted in her own life. She had tried to love before, but she found it extremely hard to stick with just one guy when there were so many others that were well equipped to please her.

Dominic stood by, watching her watch them. He was getting aggravated by how she was so preoccupied with man the green eyes.

"Questa stronza e una puttana," he thought to himself, saying *"This bitch is a whore"* in Italian.

Paula watched the green-eyed heart throb, kiss his wife on the forehead then leave off by himself. She looked at the direction he was going and saw the bathrooms. Smirking to herself when the guy made his way to the men's room, Paula got up from her chair.

"I'll be back," she told Dominic.

"I'll escort you," he said taking a step towards her.

"You will stay your ass here and wait until I come back! Got it?"

Without waiting for a response, Paula walked off, glancing at where the man's pose was. Neither of the three were paying attention to her. She smiled mischievously at the wild, wild thoughts that bounced around inside of her head, walking her insatiable sex drive right on up again.

She looked around the outside area of the bathrooms, making sure that nobody was coming, then as sneakily as she could, Paula pushed the men's room door open and slipped inside, closing the door behind her, and locking it. The toilet in one of the stalls flushed. Paula felt her heart start racing in her chest as her fantasy came close to becoming a reality. The stall door opened up and out came Green eyes. He glanced her way as he went to wash his hands. He did a double take, then started grinning at her.

"So, you aren't in a relationship with dude that seems to be all over your every move, huh?" he asked running water over his hands then lathering them with soap.

Paula laughed.

"He's my bitch. Nothing more, but!" she said, pausing, taking a few strides towards him as he dried his hands off. "What I need is a man. A real man."

He chuckled.

"Is there a such thing as a fake man?"

"Yes, there is. A little punk ass bitch is what that is," Paula said.

She then brazenly grabbed his crotch feeling how well-endowed he was. She licked her lips and looked up at him.

"So far, you have everything I desire in a man. You are incredibly handsome, incredibly buff, obviously you are incredibly rich, and you are—"

"Incredibly married."

Paula's eyes went wide. Her lips hadn't moved. He was still grinning, cheesing his ass off. She felt a tap on her shoulder right then. Turning around, she found Green eyes' wife there with a narrowed eyes frown on her face.

"H-How did you get in here?" Paula asked, knowing that she locked the door behind her.

The woman smirked at her.

"No importa como. Lo que importa es que tu metiste con la gente equivocada mamahuevo."

"Huh?" Paula asked wondering what the hell the chick had just said.

"She said, "you fucked with the wrong people, mamahuevo," she heard Green eyes say in her ear. The next thing she knew, Paula felt a slight pinch in her neck. She jumped away, spinning around. She grabbed at her neck and saw a spec of blood on her hand, then everything started getting fuzzy.

Javi and Michelle watched Paula slowly lose consciousness. With the empty hypodermic needle in his hand, Javi grinned broadly as the little Italian chick fell to the floor.

"Damn. That worked faster than the last shit you made amor!" Javi exclaimed.

"Uh huh."

SLAP!

"OW!" Javi jumped away from his wife after her open hand stung his face up. "What the hell was that for Michelle?"

";Te lo dije antes, Javier, si algunn vez dejas que otra puta te toque otra vez, I would slap the fuck out'cha ass, motherfucker! You thought I was playin?"

Javi rubbed his face.

"No."

The door opened up just then. Javi and Michelle whipped out their matching Heckler & Koch 9mm to fire until they saw it was just Danny and ChaCha with H&K semi autos as well.

"We need to go right now!" ChaCha urged as Danny stood by the door. "Her security guards are heading this way!"

Javi gave his wife his pistol, scooped up the sleeping beauty and headed towards the door. He stopped mid-step when pounding on the door came.

"PAULINA! WHAT ARE YOU DOING IN THERE!" They heard a man yell out.

"PEEING, GODDAMMIT!" Michelle yelled trying to imitate Paula's voice.

ChaCha shot her a look. Michelle shrugged and mouthed the words *"I tried!"*

BANG! BANG! BANG!

"OPEN THE DOOR! WHOEVER IN THERE WITH PAULINA PAULMATTI, COME OUT WITH HER UNHARMED OR YOU WILL DIE!"

Michelle looked at Javi.

"Now what? There's no way out!"

"There's always a way out, young one," said the head honcho of the multi-billion-dollar cocaine family as he took a step back to the middle of the bathroom floor and pointed his gun at the door.

"You just gotta be willin' to make it out, yah mean?"

ChaCha went and stood next to her husband, pointing her thumper. Michelle joined. Javi dropped Paula on the floor, got his gun, and stood with his family ready once again to go toe-to-toe with death as they had done together so many times in the past.

Dominic pounded on the door again, yelling for Paula to revealed.

FUCK YOU, BITCH! COME GET THIS HOE!" He heard a female say from inside.

His men were all ready to breach. They gripped her pistols with both hands, eager to show off their skills. The guests that had been gathered in the main area were all ushered out by the Palazzo's own security. All that remained inside were Dominic, and the sixteen men in his crew.

"On the count of three, we go in!" Dominic told them in a hushed tone. "Do not shoot Paula, or I will shoot you! Do you understand!"

"Copy, sir," one said for all of them.

"One…two…"

BOOM! BOOM! BOOM! BOOM! BOOM! BOOM! BOOM! BOOM! BOOM! BOOM!

Blood and guts splattered all over Dominic as deafening shotgun blasts. Three hit the floor, two with massive holes in them, one without a head. The others turned to return fire, only to see that it was a tiny woman that dumping on them with the fully automatic shotgun. The bathroom door flew open at that moment. Dominic swung back around and saw the bigger of the two men rush out at him. Before he could react, his pistol met Dominic's jaw, breaking it instantly.

BOOM! BOOM! BOOM! BOOM! BOOM! BOOM! BOOM!

Sonia took down two more of the guards as Danny Valdez destroyed the head guard's jaw. She dove behind a wall as the others that still stood blew back at her. Sitting with her back to the wall, started grinning to herself geeked to be back in action.

ChaCha ran out with her husband and popped one of the shooters in the back of the head, splatting another man's face with his brains. Michelle ran out with her and Javi pistols, dumping on anyone that was not with them. Javi ran out with the sedated Paulmatti Princess in his arms. Michelle ran in front of him, leading the way to the exit while the fire fight behind them continued.

BOC! BOC! BOC! BOC! BOC!

Danny rammed his pistol into the gut of the shooter and blew his stomach through his back.

BOC! BOC! BOC! BOC! CRACK!

ChaCha exchanged fire with two others that had popped up out of nowhere, then bashed another in his temple with her cannon when he tried to rush her.

BOOM! BOOM! BOOM! BOOM! BOOM!

Sonia rolled out from her perch and sent more deer-shot shells at the guards, hitting two, but then out of nowhere, she felt the barrel of a gun touch the back of her head. She heard ChaCha scream her name just then.

121

"I've been waiting for this, you scheming bitch!"

Sonia heard the most familiar voice behind her. Refusing to believe it, she dropped and rolled onto her back, only to see a masked figure there that had a tight black catsuit on accentuated her womanly curves. The Glock in her hand was less than a foot away from Sonia's face. Through the mask's mouth hole, she could see the woman's teeth gritted. Sonia's heart dropped when she realized who she was looking at.

"I...I s-saw your body!" She gasped.

The woman smirked. "You saw a body, with no head," she told Sonia, then squeezed the trigger over and over and over again.

Danny and ChaCha were running out of ammo. Security from the Palazzo continued rushing in, shooting pistols and sub-machine guns at them. They both took over around the wall closest to them, narrowly avoiding getting hit. They heard the loud blasts of the shotgun again and saw two more guards get hit.

"Yeah, Sonia! That's that G-shit I'm talking about girl!" ChaCha silently cheered.

Just as bullets flew in her and her husband's direction making them duck, ChaCha caught a glimpse of a masked figure whom she could easily tell was a woman sneak up on Sonia.

"Diesel!" she panicked as Sonia flipped over onto her back and had the woman's pistol put right in her face.

Danny looked, wincing as shrapnel from a bullet slamming into the wall by his head hit him in his face.

"SONIAAA!" ChaCha screamed in panic taking aim at the masked woman.

BOCKA! BOCKA! BOCKA! BOCKA! BOCKA!

ChaCha screamed in shock as the woman fired repeatedly, putting so many slugs into Sonia face that most of her head blew off.

BOC! BOC! BOC! BOC! BOC!

Danny shot at the woman, hitting her square in the chest, but the bullets only knocked her back.

"Fuck! She's armored!" Danny realized.

The woman looked their way, stuck up a middle finger, then she took off running. ChaCha was frozen. Seeing Sonia laid out like that after having known the Persian diamond expert for so long hurt her heart. She could hear shooting still, but she couldn't move. Her eyes filled with tears blurring her vision.

"Mena, come on! We gotta go!" Danny urged, after he created enough of a window to make their escape.

He grabbed his wife by the hand, yanked her up, and together, they ran for the exit, dumping at anyone behind them. They made it outside to the Jaguar SUV that Danny drove them there in and got up out of there, not once hearing or seeing a cop car as they got ghost.

Chapter 14

Eric was fuming. Bunz was in tears. LaLa and Deuce sensed their anguish and whimpered laying by their side. Posted outside a 4x4 Squared Mercedes G550 parked on the tarmac of the private jet section of Miami International, Eric and his wife waited for the incoming Lear to touch down.

"I'm sorry, E," wept Bunz wrapping her arms around him. "I never wanted any of this to happen. Sonia, Tanzania, Tracy, your businesses and the crews; I swear, it's like since I came back into your life shit has gone downhill. Our babies died because of me."

Eric put one arm around his wife. "Monique, you know that none of this is your fault, love. All we can do is remember that shit like this is a part of the game we been playin' for a long time." He planted a kiss on her forehead.

"But now, play time is over. I'm 'bout to murder everyone that even looks crazy when we get there."

The Lear appeared a minute later. It taxied over to where Eric, Bunz, and their dogs stood. Coming to a stop, the stairs opened up and touched the ground. Tim and Tracy emerged a second later looking like they had been to hell, came back, went there again, and almost didn't make it back. Tracy ran to her big cousin with tears in her eyes. He hugged her while Tim received a hug from Bunz.

"Well, initially we had y'all fly down to show y'all these," Eric said. He and Bunz held their hands up, revealing their wedding rings.

"Man, why we ain't get to come, E?" Tim wanted to know, feeling a little slighted.

"Yeah, cuz! How you gon' get married without us there?" Tracy added, her hands on her hips.

"It was a mutual decision y'all," Bunz said. "But don't worry; we'll have a real wedding ceremony that everyone can come to. For now, though, we have a problem to solve, and this ain't gon' be easy."

"No problems are easy to solve, fam," Tim said, "But we always make it happen."

Eric nodded. "True, except for when it comes to chasin' a ghost."

"A ghost?" Tim questioned with a raised eyebrow.

"We'll explain on the way over there, bro," Bunz told him as another jet rolled up, fueled and ready to go.

"Hold up. We're not stayin' here?" Tracy asked.

"Nope. We're going to Italy, so get some rest while we're up in the air," Eric suggested. "Because it is about to really get crazy."

Hours later, the jet landed in Milan. Waiting by a big Mercedes Sprinter, Eric, Bunz, Tim, and Tracy saw Danny, ChaCha, Macho, Yessy, and G-Baby.

"Where's Javi and his wife?" Tracy asked as they prepared to get off the jet.

"Showin' that little cum-dumpster how to guard someone without twenty goofy ass clowns with guns," Bunz told her.

Deboarding the Lear, Eric, his posse, and the dogs were greeted by the Valdez clan. Macho filled them all in on what had happened, adding in a few things that had not been known, which shocked the four of them.

"Let's go!" Eric urged, ready to go end it all.

They all got into the Sprinter and headed off joined by two black vans when they got to the exit.

Two and a half hours later out in desolate lands, the driver turned the Sprinter down a dirt path road that was nearly invisible due to trees lining the sides of the two-way highway. Tailed by the two vans, the Sprinter driver arrived at the old farmhouse, half a mile back from the road. Standing out front of the house was Javi, his sister Evelyn, and their brother Xavier, along with Xavier's wife Kenzie, and his two baby mommas Vanessa and Nena. The Sprinter hadn't even come to a complete stop before Bunz yanked the door handle, opened the door, and jumped out, running like an angry track star towards the house. Deuce was right on her bumper, sticking with her as he'd done from day one, while his pregnant mate lacked speed due to her extra weight.

"Where is she?" Bunz demanded a few feet from where the rest of the Valdez clan stood.

"Gift wrapped for you right inside," Javi told her.

Bunz ran up the stairs and pushed her way inside the old wood house with Deuce behind her. There in the middle of the bare living room was Paula Paulmatti tied to a chair, gagged with duct tape over her lips. Standing next to her was Michelle with a 12-gauge pump in her hands. Bunz saw nothing but red when she looked at the woman who had killed her babies and Andrea. She rushed her like an angry bull and attacked, swinging hard, fast, vicious punches that sent Paula and the chair flying backwards.

Eric was right behind LaLa as she ran into the house to a barking Deuce, and a furious Bunz. The others entered behind him. The mob of Jamaicans that had been in the van were ordered by Danny to post around the house, eyes open, fingers wrapped around their triggers, ready to shoot any unannounced visitors that might happen to pull up.

He saw his wife beating the shit out of Paula. Through her, Eric felt the heavy load slowly falling off of his chest. He rooted for his woman, cheered loudly for her. Bunz socked her up so hard that she felt like her own fists would soon break. Paula was fucked up. Face swollen, nose broke, eyes nearly shut; she screamed, but the tape prevented any sounds from escaping her lips. She whimpered, pain ricocheting inside of her skull, her brain pulsating like a subwoofer was in her head.

Bunz was pulled up from the floor by her husband when he saw how close she, herself, was close to breaking.

"You got her bae. Relax," he said to her, pulling her into his arms.

Bunz burst into tears, sobbing loudly. Deuce and LaLa went to her side in attempts to comfort Bunz. Macho, his ladies, and his other family stood by. Tim and Tracy stepped up and embraced Bunz. Losing the twins had a horrible effect on all of them, but Bunz having carried them in her stomach for nearly nine months; she had been hurting the worst. They were her first born, created by the realest love she could ever ask for. Michelle walked up just then. She tapped Bunz's shoulder. Bunz turned her head around and saw that Michelle had a sharp machete in her hand.

"Finish that bitch. She took E Jr. and Baby Mo-Mo from you, so take that bitch's head off and throw it in the garbage."

Bunz took the machete into her hands, gripping the wooden handle tightly. She walked back towards the bloody and swelled up Italian, ready to cut the girl's head clean off. Paula through her swollen eyes saw Bunz standing over her with the deadly chopper. Bunz clenched her teeth and started raising the machete up over her head. Eric and the others watched as Bunz got ready to deliver the death blow. Then suddenly, Paula started cackling. She laughed, laying on the floor, tied up, seconds away from dying by decapitation. She laughed at Bunz. Her laughter turned into hysterical laughter. Infuriated, Bunz reached down and snatched the tape away from Paula's mouth.

"OW! THAT HURT, BITCH!" she snapped.

"Don't worry. This won't hurt a bit," Bunz said and raised the machete up again.

"If you kill me, you'll never see your precious babies again," Paula then said staring right into Bunz's eyes.

Bunz froze. Eric froze. Tim, Tracy, and the others all furrowed up.

"Yeah, bitch. You heard right," Paula said with a bloody smile. "Your little ones are not dead. I sent ya parts from other babies that were already dead."

Bunz had no clue what to say, nor what to believe. Eric walked up to her side and glared down at the girl, ready to beat her face in himself.

"I can see you only partially believe me, so I'll get you proof of life. Tell one of these mutt motherfuckers to make a video call to this number, and you'll see."

Michell stepped up as Paula gave the number. She entered it into her phone and handed it over to Bunz and Eric. Paula smirked as she watched curiosity killed the cat facial expressions grow on their mugs. Bunz and Eric waited for the video call to be answered. After five rings the screen changed and revealed the inside of a bedroom.

"H-Hello?" stammered Bunz.

The screen moved to the left, just then. A face came into view. Bunz and Eric gasped in shock when they saw her.

"Andrea!" exclaimed Bunz, stupefied beyond belief.

Eric was completely speechless. Hearing her name, Tim ran over to them and looked at the screen. The second he saw Andrea's face; he nearly lost it.

"Hey, Bunz, Eric, and Tim!" Andrea said with the fakest smile ever. "Nice to see you all together looking happy without me."

"H-How are you...we saw your body!" Bunz said still the only one that been able to talk.

Andrea laughed. "You know. It's funny. Sonia said the same thing before I blew her brains out all over the floor."

Eric's eyes narrowed into thin slits. He so badly wished he could reach into the phone and strangle the bitch to death.

"All you saw was a headless corpse that my sister and I made look like mine." Andrea laughed again. "Dummies.

Paula started laughing then. Tracy ran over to her and field goal, kicked her in the face.

"SHUT THE FUCK UP, BITCH!" she screamed as Paula cried out in pain.

"FUCK YOU!" Paula screamed back, despite her head pounding now.

"Sounds like you all finally caught Paulina," Andrea continued. "I imagine that she's bleeding and probably in a lot of pain. Oh, by the way, Tim. How's that horse tooth bitch that I shot in the ass while she was sucking your dick?"

Tim stared at her. Tears had fallen from his bloodshot red eyes. His jaw muscles flexed as he grinded his teeth with anger.

"Aw. What's the matter? She can't poop out her booty hole anymore. I bet it's gonna really stink when the wounds start festering."

"Andrea...Where are my kids!" Bunz demanded to know as both her eyes and Eric's welled with tears.

"Hmm...let me see...ooh Eric Jr! Monique! Where are yoouu!" Andrea called out.

"Oh! There you are! Hiii. My precious little angels! Say hi to mommy and daddy!"

The camera moved from Andrea's face to the bed where Eric Jr, and his twin sister Monique laid on a blanket with toys around them. Bunz shrieked when she saw that her infant twins really were alive. Eric's eyes went so wide that they looked like they would pop out of their sockets. Tim and Tracy were stunned. The Valdez clan having heard it all were beyond happy to hear that the little boy and girl were not dead, but having been through faked deaths, kidnapping, and so many other devasting tribulations, they were hardly surprised.

"So, this is what's going to happen."

The camera went back to Andrea's face.

"You are going to release my sister, and I will give you the babies. If my sister suffers any more harm, these two will die, and I will keep popping up everywhere you go."

"Okay! I just want my kids!" Bunz said, readily agreeing to make the trade.

Eric wanted to see Paula's head sliced off, but he wanted his family back together again more. Andrea told them where to go to, and to be there in one hour with Paula in the condition she was in, not worse. The video call ended a second later.

"You sure about this Bunz?" Tim asked not sure he trusted it. "This could be a trap."

"I do not give a fuck! I will die if I have to, to get my son and daughter back! Somebody get that bitch out of that chair and let's go!"

Eric, Bunz, LaLa, Deuce, along with Tim, Tracy, and the Valdez clan all boarded luxury helicopters and flew east to the city that floated on water. When they arrived in Venice, they touched down and followed Andrea's directions, keeping Paula under their control by threat of high-powered stun gun in Michelle's hand, and by two sets of sharp teeth.

Heading through the narrow walkways that weaved in and out through the stylish old century homes, with so many waterways filled with boat docks and everything from row boats, to small powerboats, and slightly bigger touring boats, Eric and Bunz felt like they had dove into the old movie *Tomb Raider*.

It was a complex, yet elegant-looking city. The people there could tell that the large mob were not from there. Paula was so badly wanted to shout for someone to help her, but she kept hearing Bunz words in her ears…

"If you so much as fart too loud, I am going to fry yo' ass until popcorn comes out of yo' ears. I dare you to try me, bitch."

Paula knew one thing about the citizens of most Italian cities…They were not fans of mobsters, nor those related to mobsters by blood, and that went quadruple for Italian cops.

They arrived at the tall 3-story house that Andrea had directed them to. The door opened as Eric took the first step onto the stone step porch with his wife and their killers right behind them. Tim and Tracy watched the many windows of the house, while the Valdez goons and their Jamaican army kept their eyes on everything else. A man the size of a Sub-Zero refrigerator appeared in the doorway. He was bald and wearing a Versace tracksuit with the matching sneakers. "Welcome," he said with a sly grin. "I have orders for only Bunz to enter, nobody else. Oh, of course, Miss Paulmatti too."

Bunz stepped forward with Paula ahead of her. LaLa eager to go, started barking and growling while Deuce's eyes stayed locked onto the man.

"Hold up, hold up," Eric said walking forward ahead of Bunz and Paula, the dogs following along with Tim and Tracy.

The man held his hand out to stop them.

"Hey! I said only—"

Eric shot forward and grab the man's arm, and before the guy could react, Eric delivered a knee so hard to the man's groin that it made him shit on himself. He buckled and fell to the floor, crying and cursing, balled up in a fetal position. Eric wasted no time in patting the man, finding his 9mm tucked into the back waistline of his pants.

"You're gonna get your babies killed," Paula said to him.

SMACK!

Bunz gave her a hard open hand.

"Shut the fuck up, bitch!"

They stormed the house then. All of them, with the exception of the Rastas. The dreadheads stayed posted outside on security.

The house was old world luxurious with many rooms. Bunz and Eric forced Paula ahead of them, the barrel of the 9mm at the back of her head.

Tim and Tracy, both ready to die if they had to, armed themselves with knives from the kitchen while Macho, Yessy, G-Baby, Michelle, Javi, Xavier, Evelyn, Gloria. ChaCha, and Danny were ready for a good old fashion brawl since getting guns in when they arrived in Italy had proven to be impossible.

They searched high and low for Andrea and the twins. Paula made snooty comments, teasing and taunting them.

POW! ZZZZZZZZZZ!

Michelle zapped her after getting fed up with her mouth. She kept shocking her until the putrid odors that started filling the air made everyone wrinkle their noses.

"Daaamn!" Macho busted out laughing at his younger cousin-in-law once Michelle quit stunning Paula. "Lil cuz just literally shocked the shit out that bitch, yo! Homiez!"

Paula laid twitching in a puddle of her own liquified excrement. Eric and Bunz went to grab her until they heard Andrea's voice.

"Now is that really the type of shit y'all should be doin' to my sister when she willfully kept these two little ones alive when we all know that she could have let them be snake food?"

They all heard the voice, but nobody saw her. Eric and Bunz looked around frantically. Tim saw a camera on the corner with a red light on it. He pointed it out to them all.

"Hi Timmy Tim Tim! You're lookin' real good, baby! Why don't you leave the losing team and fuck with a winner?"

Tim gave no reply. He stayed where he was, wishing to have the chance to smash Andrea's face in. Next to him, Tracy was thinking the same thing…as everyone else.

"WHERE ARE MY KIDS, YOU DIRTY BITCH!" Bunz screamed.

Eric was so pissed that his demon red eyes had filled with tears. He was shaking from how angry he was.

"You're calling me dirty, Bunz? You fucking used me to lure my sister to you! I didn't even know that the bitch was my sister!"

"H-Hey!" Paula stammered, hearing Andrea's words while she remained laid out in her own shit.

"SHUT UP, PAULA!" Andrea shouted, then she got back to Bunz. "Now! This is what I want! Bring your ass up here to the roof, and we're gonna handle this like real gangsters!"

Bunz looked at the camera.

"Say less, bitch."

"And if you come up here with anyone but my stupid ass sister, your babies will learn to swim waaay before they're old enough! Got it?"

"I am not lettin' you go up there alone, Mo-Mo," Eric said as Bunz went to grab Paula by her hair.

Paula screamed as Bunz dragged her behind her towards the stairs.

"Just… take care of them, E," Bunz said looking at him. "Take care of our kids. I love you."

"Monique! It could be a trap bae!" Eric warned, terrified to lose his woman and his babies.

"Eric. I will not let either of these bitches chump me. I'm gonna go up on this roof, I'm gonna beat Andrea's ass until she shits on herself too! Then, we'll get our babies, go home, and have a real wedding. That's how this is gonna go," Bunz declared.

He watched his wife drag the crying, shitty Paulmatti princess up the stairs to where the door to the roof was. He watched Bunz open the door and step out, pulling Paula behind her. Then the door closed. ChaCha walked up to Eric and touched his shoulder.

"She'll be okay, papa. Bunz is a mother on a mission; those type of ladies do not fail," she told him.

Eric sighed to himself. Still gripping the pistol in his hand, he willed himself to trust that his woman had it, and that she would be okay.

"Ten minutes...you got ten minutes Monique to break them bitches down, then I'm comin' up there..." he thought to himself, counting the time from the last word of his thoughts.

"Yo bro," Macho walked up to Eric and embraced him in a brotherly manner.

"Bunz got this. Have faith in ya' lady because she is truly a G. On my dead Homiez."

Eric nodded. "Yeah. She most definitely is, fam," he agreed, though he knew in all of the years he had been a dope boy, a goon, and a killer...being a certified gangster wasn't always enough to make it home.

Chapter 15

Bunz stepped out on to the roof still with Paula's hair gripped tightly in her hand. The second she closed the door, she saw Andrea close to the other side of the roof by the ledge, and next to her Bunz saw a baby crib. Her heart nearly leapt out of her chest when she saw both Eric Jr, and Monique standing on their own feet inside holding on to the wooden posts lining the crib.

"My babies!" she said tearing up with joy, yet so much pain that they had been alive, all this time, and that she had given up finding them.

Bunz let Paula's hair go and attempted to run to her kids, but Andrea stopped her in her tracks when she upped a Beretta and pointed it at her.

"I would not take another step, dude," Andrea told her glaring at her venomously.

Bunz upper lip curled as her blood boiled. She stared daggers at Andrea wishing that God would drop his hand and smash the bitch.

"Paula! Get the fuck up and get over here!" she demanded.

Paula managed to get herself up. She shot Bunz a look then turned to go to her sister, but then with a quickness, she pivoted back, hand open, and went to swing on Bunz. Having saw it coming from a mile away, Bunz ducked and countered with a jab to Paula's sternum knocking the wind out of her.

"AYE!" Andrea started walking towards them, gun still trained on Bunz's face. "DO IT AGAIN! I DARE YOU, BITCH!"

She stopped four feet away from Bunz, her hand shaking from how bad she wanted to shoot her. Paula got upright, holding her stomach, taking deep labored breaths to replace the wind in her lungs that Bunz had taken from her.

"Eew! Dude, you shit yourself?" Andrea asked with disgust when she saw the back of Paula's dress.

"Hey!" Paula whipped her head around and glared at her sister. "Don't worry about me! Just shoot this bitch and be done with it! She killed our fucking father dammit."

"The father that abandoned your mother, Andrea," Bunz threw in.

"SHUT UP!" Andrea pointed her gun at Bunz's face again. "DON'T YOU EVER SAY ANYTHING ELSE ABOUT MY MOM, YOU SLIMY BITCH!"

"You're real touch with that gun in your hand. Don't forget who made you like that, shortie!"

"Oh, I didn't believe that bitch! You can also believe that you created a monster that is crazier than you!"

Bunz held up her hand and made gestures with it, calling Andrea a 'talker'.

"Gangsters don't do all that talkin' you doin', lil mama. Whenever you ready, come get these hands, bitch," Bunz told her.

Andrea handed Paula her gun and demanded for her to shoot anyone that showed up uninvited. From the crib, Bunz could hear her babies shouting. She looked in their direction and saw that they were looking her way, hopping up and down as they recognized their mother. In a flash, a millisecond before she looked back at Andrea, she was met by the furious fist of the used and abused illegitimate daughter of Barry Paulmatti.

CRACK! CRACK! CRACK! BINK!

Andrea caught her with four fast ones that had Bunz flying backwards landing on her ass.

"YEAH! YES! HAAA!" Paula shouted, as Andrea jumped on top of Bunz and went apeshit, swinging fast, flooding Bunz, overwhelming her with such speed and power.

"WHOOP THAT BITCH, GET HER! WHOOP THAT BITCH, GET HER 'DREA!"

Bunz put her arms up to block her face. Andrea outsmarted her and shot her head down as hard as she could, head-butting Bunz. She caught Bunz's forehead and dazed her.

"COME ON BITCH!" Andrea shouted punching Bunz up again.

The next punch Andrea thew, Bunz caught her hand and yanked her arm which made Andrea fly forward. Bunz shot her head up and head-butted her right in her nose.

"AAGGHH! FUCKING BITCH!" Andrea screamed holding her nose as it throbbed.

Bunz shot a hard jab up and linked Andrea making her head snap upwards. Andrea fell sideways as her bell rang. Bunz went to grab her but stopped when a gunshot rang out and the surface just inches away from her head exploded.

"ANDREA! GET UP! COME ON!" Paula yelled running over to where they both were laid out.

Eric Jr. and Monique were crying now. They saw their mother fighting, then the loud gunshot scared them to tears. Andrea got up, legs woozy, barely holding her up as the world spun her faster than a public defender did his most broke clients.

"Uh huh. Yeah bitch." Paula pointed the gun at Bunz's face, finger wrapped around the trigger. "I told you and your dumbass family...I am untouchable!" Paula then declared.

Bunz refused to beg for her life. She looked right up into Paula's eyes and welcomed her to pull the trigger, knowing that at the end of the day, she died trying to save her kids like a real mother did.

***

"Fuck! MONIQUE!" shouted Eric once he heard the gunshot. Without waiting he shot up the stairs, running full speed like a running back hellbent on scoring the winning touchdown that would lead the team to a Super Bowl victory. LaLa and Deuce were right on his heels, while Tim, Tracy, and the Valdez posse hurried behind them.

Eric rammed his heavy muscular frame against the door one good time and knocked it right off the hinges. He immediately saw Paula pointing a pistol down at his wife's face. Before he could up and point his, Paula beat him to it, taking aim at him and firing.

BOCKA! BOCKA! BOCKA! BOCKA! BOCKA!

He ducked back just in the nick of time as bullets whizzed by his head and hit the doorway. Tim and Tracy ducked when he shouted for them to back up.

"BUNZ! I'M HERE, BABY!" he shouted as Paula and Andrea took off running in the other direction.

Eric then saw the baby crib with his son, and his daughter in it crying in fear of all the chaos.

BOCKA! BOCKA! BOCKA! Click. Click. Click.

"FUUUUCK!," he heard Paula shout after she ran out of bullets.

Eric jumped up then.

"Ooooo, yo' ass is mine, bitch!" he said to himself and started dumping at the two, running to his own woman to help her up.

***

"GO! GO!" Andrea shouted when Eric ran towards where Bunz still laid, shell-shocked from coming so close to death while firing at them.

"THERE'S NOWHERE TO GO STUPID ASS BITCH!" Paula yelled back. "GRAB THE BABIES! COME ON!"

Andrea grabbed her sister's hand and forcefully yanked her with her. She ran towards the ledge of the building.

"ANDREEEEAAAA! NOOOOO!" Paula screamed as Andrea pulled to the end of the building and jumped.

"Holy shit!"

Eric got Bunz up, then ran towards where Andrea had yanked her sister over the edge of the building. Bunz ran with him, cutting right to her babies screaming with relief when she made it to them.

"Oh my God!" My babies!" she cried picking them both up and coddling them.

Eric reached the end of the roof and looked over. He saw the ripples in the water of Venice's Grand Canal where Andrea and Paula had just plunged into the water. People that been walking along the docks and the little bridge linking sections were all looking in shock, a few of them screaming with panic.

Seconds later, Eric saw the two resurface and start swimming towards one of the docks.

"Hell no! Fuck that shit!" he said and pointed his gun at them.

He was about to fire when he saw Andrea pull herself up on a slow-moving powerboat. Paula swam to her and pull herself on. The occupants of the boat attempted to fight the intruders off when they got on jack boat mode. Andrea knocked the old man that had been piloting the little boat over the side with a punch. The two older women jumped ship before she and Paula could get to them. Eric took aim at Andrea's head and got ready to put one in the top of her head when he heard everyone behind him shouting Bunz's name.

***

"Oh my God, I love you. I love you. I love youuu!" Bunz cried hugging her twins tightly to her chest.

They both cried in her arms, shaking with fear. Her heart hurt so much, but she was overjoyed to have them back in her arms. Tim and Tracy were at her side. LaLa and Deuce jumped around, both of them excited themselves that their baby humans were back.

Bunz noticed that Eric wasn't right there with her, rejoicing about their twins' safety. She looked over and saw him looking over the roof's leg, aiming his pistol. She could also hear panicking and screaming down below mixed with splashing water. She heard Andrea then, shouting for Paula to hurry up.

"Hold my babies," Bunz said to Tim and Tracy.

They obeyed her. Tim took Eric Jr. and Tracy took Monique.

"Come on, Bunz! We can still catch them!" Michelle said to her, taking her hand to pull her back towards the doorway.

Bunz yanked away from her. She looked at where her husband was still attempting to get a shot off.

"Fuck that. These bitches are not getting away," Bunz said then steeling her heart…She took off running for the roof's end with no fear in her at all.

***

He turned around just in time to see his wife running like an Olympic jumper.

"Oh shit…bae…what are…NOOO!" he shouted seconds before Bunz got to the ledge and jumped.

"BUNZ!" Eric shouted.

LaLa and Deuce followed right behind her. The three plunged into the Grand Canal making a big splash.

"AYE, E!" hollered Macho.

"I TOLD YOU BUNZ IS A GANGSTA, MY NIG!" Macho shouted.

Chuckling, Eric tucked his pistol, then he took the dive himself, feet pointed down, deep breath in his lungs, no fear in his heart as he dropped like a rock from the three stories up to the wide Venice inner city waterway.

Chapter 16

Paula laughed and cheered as Andrea put the little powerboats throttle to max and sped through the busy waterway. She nearly caused a crash every few seconds with small gondolas and tourist boats. Andrea put her sights on the end of the Grand Canal, and in minutes reached the open waters of the Golfo di Venezia.

"YEEEEAAAAHH! WOOOO!" Paula shouted up to the sky. "UNTOUCHABLE, BIIATCH!"

Remaining focused, Andrea kept eyes looking forward, as she navigated the waters. She had absolutely no intention of stopping until she reached dry land somewhere. The jig was up; all had been revealed, and there were no cards to play. Secretly, Andrea was terrified. Bunz was surely going to come after her, and so was Tim, and Tracy, and the massive mob of Caribbean gangsters that she knew so much about. Whom Andrea was worried about more…was Eric. He was the beast that had turned Bunz and Tim and Tracy into goons. He was killing, and she had participated in the abduction in the two most precious things in their lives.

As Andrea throttled the little boat further towards the Adriatic Sea, and her sister continued cheering and talking shit, memories of how good Bunz had been to her started flooding her mind. She had literally been nothing back before Bunz scooped her up, after the mass shooting at the restaurant she had been a rodie-poo chef in, walking along Geneva who turned out to be Bunz in disguise.

Bunz had taken her into her home with Eric Jr. and Monique. She had given her confidence that she never actually had, and it had meant so much to Andrea. The stacks of cash she got, the special edition Range Rover, the ridiculously expensive wardrobe Bunz had given her were the nicest and most extravagant things she had ever gotten in her entire life. The more she thought about the whole reason that Bunz had taken her in, the more Andrea had to accept that Bunz was a mother, and a queen of a King that had her kingdom destroyed and was hellbent on rebuilding it with her own hands. Andrea knew that she would have did the same thing if a bitch shot the love of her life down in front of her, and snatched her up, issuing threats to give her a C-section and put her babies in a microwave, and force her to eat them.

Tim popped into her mind. Tim. She had loved him, and he had loved her. Even though he was on Bunz's side, Andrea knew he had been in love with her. She had been able to feel it, and Andrea had fallen in love with Eric Jr. and Monique, and LaLa, and Deuce so hard that it brought tears to her eyes that it was now all over with.

"YES! YES! YEEES! HOLY SHIT! HE DID IT! HE DID IT! HE FUCKING DID IT!" Paula suddenly started shouting.

Andrea glanced over at her sister and saw that her sister had found an iPhone and was looking at whatever was on the screen.

"ANDREA! TRUMP WON! HAAAA! YES! SUCK IT, KAMALA, YOU FUCKING…WHATEVER THE HELL YOU ARE! TRUMP WORLD ORDER! LET'S GOOOOO!"

At that moment, Andrea felt her blood begin heating up. Hearing her sister, whom only recently did she find out was her sister, talk about such a dickhead that shouldn't even be alive, like he was to be hailed as king of the world, made her develop all sorts of regrets. She had participated in holding two babies from their parents, two babies that she still loved dearly, all because Paula had successfully made her feel like Bunz had committed the ultimate betrayal when she had planned to use her to get at Paula. The more Andrea thought about it, the more she realized that if she was seeking vengeance for the murder of a man that was her everything, she would stop at nothing to make it happen, which definitely would include befriending and using whoever would get her to who done it!

"SIS! TRUMP WON, BIATCH! DOWN WITH THE BROKE ASS PEOPLE! UP WITH THE RICH AND SHINY PEOPLE!" Paula shouted as she waved her phone around her head.

"Shut the fuck up, man! Damn!" Andrea snapped angrily.

Paula's excited smile dropped clean off her face. She looked at Andrea with furrowed brows.

"What the hell is your problem, dude?" Paula asked her with a major attitude.

"You! We just pissed off a family of fucking killers that nobody has ever beaten, and you over there shoutin' and cheering for a racist, booty grabbing prick!" yelled Andrea, still focusing her eyes ahead of them ignoring that Paula was over in her seat staring at her.

"First off," Paula kicked back turning her chair so that she was facing Andrea. "Fuck the Valdez family! They bleed like any other humans! Secondly, if he didn't grab your booty then what the fuck do you give a shit about the bitches whose butt he did grab! Third! Who cares if he's racist! You are white! So is he!"

"I DON'T CARE! I GREW UP IN FUCKING SHELTERS WITH BLACK PEOPLE AND LATINOS, PAULA!"

"Sucks for you; I didn't have that issue! I lived in mansions and ate steaks for school lunch! I do not give a motherfuck about poverty!"

Andrea was livid. The devastation she had seen in her time was enough to get anyone to see the big picture. People who didn't see it didn't want to. Andrea despised that.

"I should've killed you when I had the chance," she said to herself, but it was loud enough that Paula heard her.

"You ungrateful bitch!" Paula growled. "I could have killed you when I took your stupid ass from your little hotel meeting!"

"Fuck you! You know what…I'm gonna hand deliver you to Bunz and Eric like I should've done a long time ago!"

As Andrea whipped the steering wheel to the left to turn and go back, Paula screamed manically.

"YOU FUCKING BIIITCH!" Paula shouted, jumping up from her seat and charging at Andrea.

She swung a hard right and caught Andrea in her jaw while Andrea held onto the steering wheel trying to keep control of the boat. Paula swung viciously, punching Andrea up like she was a punching bag made of meat. Andrea let go of the wheel and with her left hand, she stiff-armed Paula as hard as she could in her face. Considerably smaller and lighter than Andrea, Paula went flying backwards landing on her ass. Andrea gasped when she saw a boat speeding in their direction. From nearly a quarter mile away, Andrea could see those long gold dreadlocks that she knew all too well.

"BUNZ! BUNZ!" she yelled throwing her hands up high as she could waving frantically.

Paula gasped, hearing her sister shouting that name. She looked around the little boat for anything she could use. She had no intentions of letting Andrea deliver her to sure death. She then laid her eyes on something that would be sure to get her illegitimate sister's attention. Paula slithered her way over towards it and took it off the hook. She stood and with her teeth gritted, she called her sister's name.

"BUUUUNZ!" Andrea shouted as she and the other boat closed in on each other.

"HEY! ANDREA!"

She heard Paula call her. At first, she glanced in Paula's direction thinking the shorter chick was about to swing on her again. But then, seeing something shiny glinting in her peripheral view, Andrea turned her head all the way, and saw that her sister was holding a harpoon, poised to hurl it right at her.

***

Eric saw the two inside the boat going at it as Bunz continued steering the powerboat she had swiped with LaLa and Deuce right towards Paula and Andrea. From where they were, a few hundred yards away still, Eric saw Paula pick up something long with a shiny point at the front end, pointing it at Andrea.

"Oh shit," he said to himself just as Paula hurled it at Andrea hitting her right in the center of her face.

"Son of a bitch!" Bunz cursed as she and Eric both saw Andrea fall backwards into the water.

***

Paula launched the harpoon as hard as she could. Before Andrea could get out of its way, the sharp tip penetrated her face and pushed out the back of her head, killing her instantly. Andrea's lifeless body fell overboard and hit the water, blood spilling out of her head into the water like the oil leak of the Exxon Valdez.

She ran to grab the steering wheel right as the boat started to lose control. Taking the wheel in her hands, Paula got it back under control, but as she looked up, she saw the boat that Bunz was in heading right for her, closing in very fast.

"Oh, sh-sh-shit!" she gasped as she and Bunz got so close that she could see the fire in Bunz's eyes and Eric's.

"JUMP!" Bunz shouted to Eric and their dogs.

Seconds before the two boats collided head on, the four jumped into the water, escaping the massive fireball resulting from the crash. Bunz and Eric resurfaced in seconds. LaLa and Deuce right with them. It rained powerboat parts and debris. Chunks of what was left of the two boats burned while still floating. Bunz and Eric looked all around for Paula, but she was nowhere in sight. Bunz took a deep breath and went under, searching underwater for the bitch. A few hundred feet away she saw Paula's white dress. She swam towards her, praying that she was alive so that she could kill her.

"MONIQUE! AYE!" Eric's heart dropped when his wife dove under to find Paula.

LaLa and Deuce treaded water next to him until Bunz went under. Deuce shot down and dog paddled to catch up.

"Goddammit!" Eric said then took a deep breath and dove down into the water to join the fight.

***

Paula's eyes opened the second she felt a pair of hands grab her. She locked eyes with Bunz and instantly went into survival mode. Bunz headbutted Paula hard enough that even underwater the impact made her nose start to bleed. Bunz cocked back and socked Paula once, then twice, then a third time, splitting her bottom lip open. Deuce appeared and sank his teeth into Paula's shoulder, clamping down on it as hard as he could. Hundreds of bubbled screams came out of Paula's mouth as the pain crippled her. Then, LaLa came and chomped down on Paula's arm, biting into it so hard that she cracked the bone. Eric grabbed Bunz and pulled her up the surface before she killed herself while trying to kill Paula.

"LET ME GO! LET ME GO! I'M NOT DONE WITH THAT BITCH, E," Bunz cried trying to pull away and dive back down.

"BUNZ, CHILL OUT!" Eric yelled, seeing that his wife had gone insane. "YOU GOT HER ALREADY! SHE'S DONE FOR!"

Just then, the surface of the water broke. LaLa and Deuce had pulled Paula up. She bled from so many bite wounds along with her nose and her lip. She thrashed and kicked making water splash all over. LaLa and Deuce obeyed when Eric called them off.

"NOO! SHE HAS TO DIE, ERIC! LET ME FUCKING GOOOO!" Bunz screamed hysterically.

Paula in a delirious state, started laughing at Bunz, taunting her as she bled out into the sea.

"Y-You c-c-can't kill me, b-bitch! I'm unt-t-touchable! Haa! I am in-touch—"

Before Paula could finish her statement, the long jaw with huge sharp teeth of a massive sperm whale shot up through the water where Paula had been thrashing like an injured seal. The whale snapped Paula up as it shot all the way up in the air, clamping its jaws shut, crushing her to death in its meat ripping teeth.

"OOHH SHIIT! WHAT THE FUCK!" Eric shouted, grabbing his wife and pulling her to him just as the ten-ton whale crashed back down into the water and smacked the surface with its enormous tail.

Paula was gone from their sight being dragged down to the depths of the Italian sea, swallowed by the whale whole, not a thing left of her except the crimson blood that stained the sea waters. Eric was stunned speechless, still holding his wife while LaLa and Deuce continued treading water at their side.

"Hoooooly shit!" he finally was able to say.

"MOTHERFUUCKEER!" Bunz suddenly screamed as the whale resurfaced a distance away from where they were. "YOU FAT PIECE OF SHIT! THAT WAS MY KILL, BITCH! BRING YO' BITCH ASS BACK HERE! I'LL KILL YOOOUUU!"

"Bunz," Eric said turning her to face him. "Do you realize you're cussin' a whale out?"

"Fuck that whale! And Fuck Trump! Fuck Paula! Fuck Andrea! Fuck Italy! AAAAHHH!" she screamed so irate with anger that she couldn't do anything but let it out.

LaLa and Deuce swam up to her, both of them whimpering. They nudged her with their noses sensing and hearing how furious that she was.

"Monique Duque Bounds?" Eric called to her, cupping her face in his hands.

"What man!" she snapped.

"I love you," he told her.

Those three words instantly made her anger dissolve. Her furious face turned into one of relief and gratitude. She managed to smile at him.

"I love you too, E," she said, her voice breaking up with a rollercoaster of emotions racing through her.

The whirring sounds of a helicopter approaching got their attention. They looked up and saw one of the big Sikarskie they had all flown to Venice on coming their way. In less than a minute later, it came to a hover above them creating powerful gusts that chopped up the waters they were floating in.

The side door slid open. Macho tossed out a long thick rope that reached all the way down to them. Eric had his wife climb up first, then he had LaLa bite down on the rope and hold while Macho pulled her all the way up. Deuce was pulled up next, then Eric climbed up. With them all safely inside with Macho, Javi, ChaCha, Michelle, and Danny up in the pilot's area; Yessy and G-Baby flew off heading back to shore.

"Maaan, y'all niggaz is cray-cray yo! On the Homiez!" Macho exclaimed, shaking his head while chuckling.

"Where's Paula at?" Michelle asked them.

"In a whale's stomach," Eric told her as he wrapped the warming blanket around Bunz and himself.

"Yo, on my raise," Danny chimed in then. "The shit y'all just did that was some *Mission Impossible* shit right there, yo. Homiez, I have never seen that type of shit in real life."

"Yo, that shit was like that part in *Jurassic World,*" Eric said still amazed at what had just happened. "When that damn flyin' thing tried to eat that British chick, and they both got ate by that giant ass thing in the water."

Macho and his family busted out laughing at Eric.

"Bae?" he said to his wife, holding her tightly in his arms while Macho and Danny rubbed the dogs with thick dry towels. "You okay?"

Bunz sighed. "I got robbed by a whale."

Eric started laughing.

"At least you got to beat that bitch up before she became food, right?" And we have our babies back; Andrea's dead; Tanzania's gonna be okay, and we got millions and businesses to get back to runnin'. I think we should realize how fortunate we are baby."

She started smiling then.

"You're right, E. We're blessed. We have good lives that we got from the mud."

"And now," ChaCha chimed in. "Y'all are about to build an empire. So, I think that this is the perfect time for you to say it E."

Bunz looked at her, then at her husband with confusion etched on her face. Eric started laughing his ass off at ChaCha, then taking the queue, he shouted it out at the top of his lungs.

"PROBLEM SOLVED...BIATCH!"

"AND FUCK TRUMP!" Bunz added. "BIATCH!"

THE END

Lock Down Publications and Ca$h Presents
Assisted Publishing Packages

Due to an increase in the price of services we have increased our prices. The prices below reflect the price increase as of 11/1/24.

BASIC PACKAGE **$699** Editing Cover Design Formatting	**UPGRADED PACKAGE** **$1000** Typing Editing Cover Design Formatting Upload eBooks to Amazon Upload Paperback to Amazon
ADVANCE PACKAGE **$1,400** Typing Editing (line editing/content) Cover Design Formatting Copyright Registration Proofreading Upload eBooks to Amazon Upload Paperback to Amazon	**LDP SUPREME PACKAGE** **$1,700** Typing Editing (line editing/content) Cover Design Formatting Copyright Registration Proofreading Set up Amazon Account Upload eBooks to Amazon Upload Paperback to Amazon Advertise on LDP's Amazon and Facebook Page

***
Other services available upon request.
Additional charges may apply

Lock Down Publications
P.O. Box 944
Stockbridge, GA 30281-9998
Phone: 470 303-9761
Email: lockdownpublications@gmail.com

Submission Guideline

Submit the first three chapters of your completed manuscript to ldpsubmissions@gmail.com. In the subject line add **Your Book's Title**. The manuscript must be in a Word Doc file and sent as an attachment. Document should be in Times New Roman, double spaced, and in size 12 font. Also, provide your synopsis and full contact information. If sending multiple submissions, they must each be in a separate email.

Have a story but no way to send it electronically? You can still submit to LDP/Ca$h Presents. Send in the first three chapters, written or typed, of your completed manuscript to:

LDP: Submissions Dept
P.O. Box 944
Stockbridge, GA 30281-9998

DO NOT send original manuscript. Must be a duplicate.
Provide your synopsis and a cover letter containing your full contact information.

Thanks for considering LDP and Ca$h Presents.

NEW RELEASES

BLOODLINE OF A SAVAGE 1-3
THESE VICIOUS STREETS 1-3
RELENTLESS GOON 1-3
BY PRINCE A. TAUHID

THE BUTTERFLY MAFIA 1-3
BY FUMIYA PAYNE

A THUG'S STREET PRINCESS 1&2
BY MEESHA

CITY OF SMOKE 3
BY MOLOTTI

GET IT IN SLUGS 1 &2
BY B. STALL

STANDING ON HER BUSINESS 1&2
BY DG SANTANA

STEPPERS 1,2&3
THE REAL BADDIES OF CHI-RAQ
BY KING RIO

THE LANE 1&2
BY KEN-KEN SPENCE

THUG OF SPADES 1&2
LOVE IN THE TRENCHES 2
CORNER BOYS
BY COREY ROBINSON

TIL DEATH 3
BY ARYANNA

CHRISTOPHER "DIESEL" HORNEZES

THE BIRTH OF A GANGSTER 4
BY DELMONT PLAYER

PRODUCT OF THE STREETS 1-3
BY DEMOND "MONEY" ANDERSON

NO TIME FOR ERROR
BY KEESE

MONEY HUNGRY DEMONS 1-2
BY TRANAY ADAMS

HUB CITY MENACE 1-3
BY J. WHITE

A THUGGISH PASSION 1&2
LAND OF DA HOOLIGANZ 1-4
KILLAZ ON STANDBY 1&2
BY IRA B.

FO'EVA ROLLIN 1&2
BY ASSA RAYMOND BAKER

THE LEVEL UP 1&3
BY LUXURY KING

Coming Soon from Lock Down Publications/Ca$h Presents

IF YOU CROSS ME ONCE 6
ANGEL V
By Anthony Fields

A THUGS STREET PRINCESS 3
By Meesha

CORNER BOYS 2
By Corey Robinson

THA TAKEOVER
By Keith Chandler

BETRAYAL OF A G 2
By Ray Vinci

SAVAGE FAMILY EMPIRE 1&2
SOULLESS GOON 1,2&3
THE DIRTY SIDE OF MONEY 1,2&3
By Prince

FOR MY ENEMY'S SAKE
AMBITIONS OF A SLIDER
FRESH OFF DA PORCH
By IRA B.

THE TRUCKLOAD 1-4
TIPPIN' THE SCALES 1-3
BAD BITCHES WIT GUNZ 3
PROBLEM SOLVED 2
By Christopher "Diesel" Hornezes

Available Now

RESTRAINING ORDER 1 & 2
By **CA$H & Coffee**

LOVE KNOWS NO BOUNDARIES 1-3
By **Coffee**

RAISED AS A GOON I, II, III & IV
BRED BY THE SLUMS I, II, III
BLAST FOR ME I & II
ROTTEN TO THE CORE I II III
A BRONX TALE I, II, III
DUFFLE BAG CARTEL I II III IV V VI
HEARTLESS GOON I II III IV V
A SAVAGE DOPEBOY I II
DRUG LORDS I II III
CUTTHROAT MAFIA I II
KING OF THE TRENCHES
By **Ghost**

LAY IT DOWN I & II
LAST OF A DYING BREED I II
BLOOD STAINS OF A SHOTTA I & II III
By **Jamaica**

LOYAL TO THE GAME I II III
LIFE OF SIN I, II III
By **TJ & Jelissa**

IF LOVING HIM IS WRONG...I & II
LOVE ME EVEN WHEN IT HURTS I II III
By **Jelissa**

PUSH IT TO THE LIMIT
By **Bre' Hayes**

PROBLEM SOLVED 3

BLOODY COMMAS I & II
SKI MASK CARTEL I, II & III
KING OF NEW YORK I II, III IV V
RISE TO POWER I II III
COKE KINGS I II III IV V
BORN HEARTLESS I II III IV
KING OF THE TRAP I II
By **T.J. Edwards**

WHEN THE STREETS CLAP BACK I & II III
THE HEART OF A SAVAGE I II III IV
MONEY MAFIA I II
LOYAL TO THE SOIL I II III
By **Jibril Williams**

A DISTINGUISHED THUG STOLE MY HEART I II & III
LOVE SHOULDN'T HURT I II III IV
RENEGADE BOYS 1-4
PAID IN KARMA 1-3
SAVAGE STORMS 1-3
AN UNFORESEEN LOVE 1-3
BABY, I'M WINTERTIME COLD 1-3
A THUG'S STREET PRINCESS 1&2
By **Meesha**

A GANGSTER'S CODE 1-3
A GANGSTER'S SYN 1-3
THE SAVAGE LIFE 1-3
CHAINED TO THE STREETS 1-3
BLOOD ON THE MONEY 1-3
A GANGSTA'S PAIN 1-3
BEAUTIFUL LIES AND UGLY TRUTHS
CHURCH IN THESE STREETS
By **J-Blunt**

CUM FOR ME 1-8
An LDP Erotica Collaboration

CHRISTOPHER "DIESEL" HORNEZES

BLOOD OF A BOSS 1-5
SHADOWS OF THE GAME
TRAP BASTARD
By **Askari**

THE STREETS BLEED MURDER 1-3
THE HEART OF A GANGSTA 1-3
By **Jerry Jackson**

WHEN A GOOD GIRL GOES BAD
By **Adrienne**

THE COST OF LOYALTY 1-3
By **Kweli**

BRIDE OF A HUSTLA 1-3
THE FETTI GIRLS 1-3
CORRUPTED BY A GANGSTA 1-4
BLINDED BY HIS LOVE
THE PRICE YOU PAY FOR LOVE 1-3
DOPE GIRL MAGIC 1-3
By **Destiny Skai**

A KINGPIN'S AMBITION
A KINGPIN'S AMBITION II
I MURDER FOR THE DOUGH
By **Ambitious**

TRUE SAVAGE 1-7
DOPE BOY MAGIC 1-3
MIDNIGHT CARTEL 1-3
CITY OF KINGZ 1&2
NIGHTMARE ON SILENT AVE
THE PLUG OF LIL MEXICO 1&2
CLASSIC CITY
By **Chris Green**

PROBLEM SOLVED 3

A GANGSTER'S REVENGE 1-4
THE BOSS MAN'S DAUGHTERS 1-5
A SAVAGE LOVE 1&2
BAE BELONGS TO ME 1&2
A HUSTLER'S DECEIT 1-3
WHAT BAD BITCHES DO 1-3
SOUL OF A MONSTER 1-3
KILL ZONE
A DOPE BOY'S QUEEN 1-3
TIL DEATH 1-3
IMMA DIE BOUT MINE 1-6
DYING FOR LIKES
By **Aryanna**

A DOPEBOY'S PRAYER
By **Eddie "Wolf" Lee**

THE KING CARTEL 1-3
By **Frank Gresham**

THESE NIGGAS AIN'T LOYAL 1-3
By **Nikki Tee**

GANGSTA SHYT 1-3
By **CATO**

THE ULTIMATE BETRAYAL
By **Phoenix**

BOSS'N UP 1-3
By **Royal Nicole**

I LOVE YOU TO DEATH
By **Destiny J**

I RIDE FOR MY HITTA
I STILL RIDE FOR MY HITTA
By **Misty Holt**

CHRISTOPHER "DIESEL" HORNEZES

LOVE & CHASIN' PAPER
By **Qay Crockett**

TO DIE IN VAIN
SINS OF A HUSTLA
By **ASAD**

BROOKLYN HUSTLAZ
By **Boogsy Morina**

BROOKLYN ON LOCK 1 & 2
By **Sonovia**

GANGSTA CITY
By **Teddy Duke**

A DRUG KING AND HIS DIAMOND 1-3
A DOPEMAN'S RICHES
HER MAN, MINE'S TOO 1&2
CASH MONEY HO'S
THE WIFEY I USED TO BE 1&2
PRETTY GIRLS DO NASTY THINGS
By **Nicole Goosby**

LIPSTICK KILLAH 1-3
CRIME OF PASSION 1-3
FRIEND OR FOE 1-3
By **Mimi**

TRAPHOUSE KING 1-3
KINGPIN KILLAZ 1-3
STREET KINGS 1&2
PAID IN BLOOD 1&2
CARTEL KILLAZ 1-3
DOPE GODS 1&2
By **Hood Rich**

THE STREETS ARE CALLING
By **Duquie Wilson**

STEADY MOBBN' 1-3
THE STREETS STAINED MY SOUL 1-3
By **Marcellus Allen**

WHO SHOT YA 1-3
SON OF A DOPE FIEND 1-4
HEAVEN GOT A GHETTO 1&2
SKI MASK MONEY 1&2
By **Renta**

GORILLAZ IN THE BAY 1-4
TEARS OF A GANGSTA 1/&2
3X KRAZY 1&2
STRAIGHT BEAST MODE 1&2
By **DE'KARI**

TRIGGADALE 1-3
MURDA WAS THE CASE 1-3
By **Elijah R. Freeman**

SLAUGHTER GANG 1-3
RUTHLESS HEART 1-3
By **Willie Slaughter**

GOD BLESS THE TRAPPERS 1-3
THESE SCANDALOUS STREETS 1-3
FEAR MY GANGSTA 1-5
THESE STREETS DON'T LOVE NOBODY 1-2
BURY ME A G 1-5
A GANGSTA'S EMPIRE 1-4
THE DOPEMAN'S BODYGAURD 1&2
THE REALEST KILLAZ 1-3
THE LAST OF THE OGS 1-3
By **Tranay Adams**

MARRIED TO A BOSS 1-3
By **Destiny Skai & Chris Green**

CHRISTOPHER "DIESEL" HORNEZES

KINGZ OF THE GAME 1-7
CRIME BOSS 1-4
By **Playa Ray**

FUK SHYT
By **Blakk Diamond**

DON'T F#CK WITH MY HEART 1&2
By **Linnea**

ADDICTED TO THE DRAMA 1-3
IN THE ARM OF HIS BOSS
By **Jamila**

LOYALTY AIN'T PROMISED 1&2
By **Keith Williams**

YAYO 1-4
A SHOOTER'S AMBITION 1&2
BRED IN THE GAME
By **S. Allen**

TRAP GOD 1-3
RICH $AVAGE 1-3
MONEY IN THE GRAVE 1-3
CARTEL MONEY 1&2
By **Martell Troublesome Bolden**

FOREVER GANGSTA 1&2
GLOCKS ON SATIN SHEETS 1&2
By **Adrian Dulan**

TOE TAGZ 1-4
LEVELS TO THIS SHYT 1&2
IT'S JUST ME AND YOU
By **Ah'Million**

PROBLEM SOLVED 3

KINGPIN DREAMS 1-3
RAN OFF ON DA PLUG
By **Paper Boi Rari**

THE STREETS MADE ME 1-3
By **Larry D. Wright**

CONFESSIONS OF A GANGSTA 1-4
CONFESSIONS OF A JACKBOY 1-3
CONFESSIONS OF A HITMAN
CONFESSIONS OF A DOPE BOY
By **Nicholas Lock**

I'M NOTHING WITHOUT HIS LOVE
SINS OF A THUG
TO THE THUG I LOVED BEFORE
A GANGSTA SAVED XMAS
IN A HUSTLER I TRUST
By **Monet Dragun**

QUIET MONEY 1-3
THUG LIFE 1-3
EXTENDED CLIP 1&2
A GANGSTA'S PARADISE
By **Trai'Quan**

CAUGHT UP IN THE LIFE 1-3
THE STREETS NEVER LET GO 1-3
By **Robert Baptiste**

NEW TO THE GAME 1-3
MONEY, MURDER & MEMORIES 1-3
By **Malik D. Rice**

CREAM 2-3
THE STREETS WILL TALK
By **Yolanda Moore**

CHRISTOPHER "DIESEL" HORNEZES

THE STREETS WILL NEVER CLOSE 1-3
By **K'ajji**

LIFE OF A SAVAGE 1-4
A GANGSTA'S QUR'AN 1-4
MURDA SEASON 1-3
GANGLAND CARTEL 1-3
CHI'RAQ GANGSTAS 1-4
KILLERS ON ELM STREET 1-3
JACK BOYZ N DA BRONX 1-3
A DOPEBOY'S DREAM 1-3
JACK BOYS VS DOPE BOYS 1-3
COKE GIRLZ
COKE BOYS
SOSA GANG 1&2
BRONX SAVAGES
BODYMORE KINGPINS
BLOOD OF A GOON
By **Romell Tukes**

CONCRETE KILLA 1-3
VICIOUS LOYALTY 1-3
BLOODY MONEY BAGS
By **Kingpen**

THE ULTIMATE SACRIFICE 1-6
KHADIFI
IF YOU CROSS ME ONCE 1-3
ANGEL 1-4
IN THE BLINK OF AN EYE
By **Anthony Fields**

THE LIFE OF A HOOD STAR
By **Ca$h & Rashia Wilson**

NIGHTMARES OF A HUSTLA 1-3
BLOOD AND GAMES 1&2
By **King Dream**

PROBLEM SOLVED 3

GHOST MOB
By **Stilloan Robinson**

HARD AND RUTHLESS 1&2
MOB TOWN 251
THE BILLIONAIRE BENTLEYS 1-3
REAL G'S MOVE IN SILENCE
By **Von Diesel**

MOB TIES 1-7
SOUL OF A HUSTLER, HEART OF A KILLER 1-3
GORILLAZ IN THE TRENCHES
OOPS CRY TOO 1&2
THE DAUGHTER OF A CARTEL BOSS
By **SayNoMore**

BODYMORE MURDERLAND 1-3
THE BIRTH OF A GANGSTER 1-4
By **Delmont Player**

FOR THE LOVE OF A BOSS 1&2
By **C. D. Blue**

KILLA KOUNTY 1-5
TENDER
By **Khufu**

MOBBED UP 1-4
THE BRICK MAN 1-5
THE COCAINE PRINCESS 1-10
STEPPERS 1-3
SUPER GREMLIN 1-4
A GANGSTA'S SON
By **King Rio**

MONEY GAME 1&2
By **Smoove Dolla**

CHRISTOPHER "DIESEL" HORNEZES

A GANGSTA'S KARMA 1-5
By **FLAME**

KING OF THE TRENCHES 1-3
By **GHOST & TRANAY ADAMS**

BAD BITCHES WIT GUNZ 1&2
PROBLEM SOLVED
By **"Christopher Diesel" Hornezes**

QUEEN OF THE ZOO 1&2
By **Black Migo**

GRIMEY WAYS 1-3
BETRAYAL OF A G
By **Ray Vinci**

XMAS WITH AN ATL SHOOTER
By **Ca$h & Destiny Skai**

KING KILLA 1&2
By **Vincent "Vitto" Holloway**

BETRAYAL OF A THUG 1&2
By **Fre$h**

COUNTDOWN OF A KILLA 1&2
SEX, MURDER AND GOD 1&2
GUNS DOWN, BOTTOMS UP 1&2
By Lo-Life

THE MURDER QUEENS 1-7
By **Michael Gallon**

FOR THE LOVE OF BLOOD 1-4
By **Jamel Mitchell**

PROBLEM SOLVED 3

HOOD CONSIGLIERE 1&2
NO TIME FOR ERROR
By **Keese**

PROTÉGÉ OF A LEGEND 1,2&3
LOVE IN THE TRENCHES 1&2
By **Corey Robinson**

THE PLUG'S RUTHLESS DAUGHTER 1&2
By **Tony Daniels**

BORN IN THE GRAVE 1-3
CRIME PAYS
By **Self Made Tay**

MOAN IN MY MOUTH
By **XTASY**

TORN BETWEEN A GANGSTER AND A GENTLEMAN
By **J-BLUNT & Miss Kim**

LOYALTY IS EVERYTHING 1-3
CITY OF SMOKE 1-3
By **Molotti**

HERE TODAY GONE TOMORROW 1&2
By **Fly Rock**

WOMEN LIE MEN LIE 1-4
FIFTY SHADES OF SNOW 1-3
STACK BEFORE YOU SPLURGE
GIRLS FALL LIKE DOMINOES
NAÏVE TO THE STREETS
By **ROY MILLIGAN**

PILLOW PRINCESS
By **S. Hawkins**

CHRISTOPHER "DIESEL" HORNEZES

THE BUTTERFLY MAFIA 1-3
SALUTE MY SAVAGERY 1&2
By **Fumiya Payne**

THE LANE 1&2
By Ken-Ken Spence

THE PUSSY TRAP 1-5
By **Nene Capri**

DIRTY DNA
By **Blaque**

SANCTIFIED AND HORNY
by **XTASY**

BOOKS BY LDP'S CEO, CA$H

TRUST IN NO MAN
TRUST IN NO MAN 2
TRUST IN NO MAN 3
BONDED BY BLOOD
SHORTY GOT A THUG
THUGS CRY
THUGS CRY 2
THUGS CRY 3
TRUST NO BITCH
TRUST NO BITCH 2
TRUST NO BITCH 3
TIL MY CASKET DROPS
RESTRAINING ORDER
RESTRAINING ORDER 2
IN LOVE WITH A CONVICT
LIFE OF A HOOD STAR
XMAS WITH AN ATL SHOOTER

www.ingramcontent.com/pod-product-compliance
Lightning Source LLC
Chambersburg PA
CBHW071220260626
47162CB00004B/1369